C000050909

HOPELESS ROMANTIC

JULIE CAPULET

When he falls, he falls *hard*.

Millie Baylin just moved to a new city to start college. Introverted and studious, she plans on spending most of her time holed up in the library working on her novel and keeping to herself. But when she gets dragged along to a school football game by her fun, football-mad new roommate, the hot alpha quarterback almost drops the ball at his very first sight of her.

Bo McCabe is saving himself. A hopeless romantic at heart, he's holding out for the real thing. As soon as he lays eyes on the shy stranger with the striking gray eyes and the angel's face, he'll stop at nothing to find out if she's the one he's been waiting for all along. Millie thinks Bo's insta-obsession is insanity and wants nothing to do with him. But Bo is determined. Because, somehow, Millie has already stolen his heart ... and he is now utterly obsessed with winning hers.

Can Bo convince Millie he's the man of her dreams?

Hopeless Romantic is a sexy standalone novella starring an obsessed hero and the love of his life (includes three hopelessly romantic HEA epilogues!). This book is a safe, feel-good, low-angst tribute to love at first sight and insta-everything (because it happened to me :).

Book 1 in the McCabe Brothers series

JULIE CAPULET ROMANCE

HOPELESS ROMANTIC
Copyright © 2019 Julie Capulet

ISBN: 9798638800154

www.juliecapulet.com

To my husband

We met in a bar. We were both ordering drinks. We started
talking. Within five minutes we knew we'd get married.
One month later, we got engaged. Two months after that,
we said our vows. That was more than ten years ago, and
each day with you only gets better. I've never had a single
moment of doubt that you are and always will be my one
and only. I loved you from that very first day.

Some people say instalove doesn't happen in real life. We
know better.

CONTENTS

Chapter One

Millie

The bus drops me next to the front entrance of the university and I walk up to the main admissions building, where I'm given a map and a bag full of booklets and welcome materials. I make my way through the crowd of people on the campus green, keeping my hat low over my eyes, using the map to try to find my way to my new dorm.

I can't believe I'm here.

College.

I never knew if I'd actually get this far. So many times along the way, college had seemed like a place *other* people went, a goal not just up among the stars, but over in someone else's galaxy. But I've made it. This is *real*. My dream, against all odds, has come true.

I graduated from high school more than a year ago, but it's taken me this long to save up enough money to get started. Desperate to get as far away from my tiny hometown in Florida as possible, I applied to four schools. *And I got in.*

This place is like a different world. More than forty thousand students go to this university. It's practically its own city, with top-ranked sports teams and space-age libraries and students from every walk of life you could imagine. It's got an energetic, optimistic vibe to it that's blowing my mind a little. The autumn air is crisp and cool. People are pink-cheeked, wearing colorful scarves, holding steaming cups of coffee and hot chocolate from a nearby coffee truck. Until two days ago, I'd never in my life been north of Atlanta. Everything about this place feels new and exciting and picture perfect. I almost feel like I belong here.

Belonging isn't something I've had a lot of experience with. I don't fit in or make friends easily. Not because I intentionally try to be an outcast, but because I'm used to keeping secrets.

But not anymore.

All my secrets have turned to dust.

Here, I'm not the poor kid with a heroin addict for a mother. Or the lonely waif who lives in a trailer park and carries Narcan in her pockets. I'm not the freaky teenage girl who wears hats and oversized jackets in August to hide myself because I live alone, or close enough. My only protector was too far gone to care.

All that is behind me now.

My mother is dead. It feels like a mercy. The needles, the wasting away, the giving up of every shred of herself just to get her next fix. I tried to save her, but she just couldn't be saved. Grief was weaved into the painful fabric of our downward spiral. Which meant that, as soon as she was gone, it was surprisingly easy to walk away. I'd already said my goodbyes to the person my mother was, a long time ago.

Now, I'm *free*. Free of the pain and sadness of my past.

Today, here—right this minute—I can start my new life.

In this mini-city of forty thousand people, I know I can find my own quiet corner, where I'll be perfectly content to watch everyone else having the time of their lives while I get to work and do what I came here to do. Kick ass, in the only way I know how.

It's a strange thing to have a knack for. As soon as I started writing stories, something clicked. When I write, I enter this fever dream. I use writing to crawl inside my own mind. To escape from reality. It helped, when I needed it most.

The coffee-scented air leads me over to the coffee truck. I stand in line. I'm wearing my usual loose jacket and my black sailor's cap that I tuck my hair into. Because I actually *need* them in this weather, which is a nice change. People still stare at me. I'm used to it. I know what I look like.

Students are clustered into groups, talking to each other, *meeting* each other. Sometimes I wonder, like now, what it would be like to be fun and outgoing. The girl behind me in line starts up bubbly conversations with a couple of random strangers, without even a hint of self-consciousness or turning red or stammering over her words, like I would. Shyness is a curse.

My backstory doesn't help, but at some point, you just have to move on. That's why I'm here, after all.

"What can I get you?" says the guy in the truck. He's staring. I pull my hat a little lower.

"One hot chocolate, please."

He smiles, making no move to get my order. "You must be a freshman. I'm sure I would have noticed you."

"Yes. I just arrived." After three days on a Greyhound bus, but I don't bother with the details.

He pours cocoa into a cardboard cup. "I'm Mason."

"Hi, Mason."

I don't offer my name in return. There's a line behind me and I really just want to get my drink so I can go and find my dorm. But Mason takes his time. "And you are?"

I relent. "Millie."

"Millie," he repeats. "I like that name."

"It's sort of old-fashioned, but it works."

His gaze roves across my face, taking its time. "Hey, there's a party at my place tonight. You should come." He scrawls a number on a napkin and hands it to me, along with my cup of hot chocolate. "Give me a call."

"I'll see. Thanks." I hand him my money card.

"It's on the house," he says. "Really. You should come. It'll be fun. I can pick you up if you need a ride."

"Hey, man," says a guy behind me in line. "How about stop trying to pick up the freshman and make us some coffee instead?"

I take that as my cue. "Thanks, Mason."

"See you tonight, hopefully," Mason calls after me, but I let myself drift into the crowd. I already know I'm not going to Mason's party. I'm not really the party-going type. Besides, I don't have time. Part of being able to afford college came from the advance money for a book I wrote last year, when I was going through the worst of ... the worst. By some miracle, I landed a literary agent, who got me a two-book deal with a major publisher. They said my writing was "heartfelt," which is true enough. The money isn't a huge amount, but it meant I could afford to start college this year, instead of waiting another year or two to save. I have no idea how I'll finish the second book by their deadline of January first, but I guess I'll figure it out. That, along with the full course load I'll be taking, means I'll basically be living in the library for the entire first semester.

I check my map, pretending I feel confident and ready to take my new world by storm. At least if I *look* like I know what I'm doing, people might actually think I do.

There's a band playing a Fleetwood Mac song in the middle of the green. Nearby, some guys are throwing a football around.

The sky is blue, with only a few high, wispy clouds. It's late afternoon. The leafy trees are vibrant shades of red and orange, with an artful smattering sprinkled across the green grass. Autumn, like I've only seen it in movies. Everything's so colorful and ... *collegiate*. Preppies, jocks, hipsters and academics are mingling, all wearing splashes of the same school colors.

Nearby, a cluster of girls are eyeing up the football jocks. These are the kinds of girls who used to make my life hell in high school. The social media-obsessed types who spend hours making sure their selfies are envy-worthy. They hate people like me: people with problems they don't want touching them and their shiny lives. Loners, who—God knows why, since I avidly try to avoid it—take attention away from them. And it's always the kind of attention I wish I wasn't getting.

I do my best to avoid them. Maybe things will be different in college.

I'm mortified when one of the jocks calls out to me and starts walking over to me. He's huge, and built like a Marvel character.

I try to steer clear but he blocks my way, so I'm forced to stop.

"Hey," he says. He's literally towering over me. I have no doubt he could break me in half if he wanted to. It's intimidating. "Are you a freshman?"

I just had this conversation, and I really don't feel like having it again. I'm not good at small talk. "Yes. And I'm on my way to my dorm, if you'll excuse me."

"You're fucking *gorgeous*," he says.

I don't know how to reply to that so I step around him and keep walking but he walks along with me.

He's persistent. "Where're you from?"

I don't want to chit-chat with this oversized stranger. "A very small town I'm sure you've never heard of."

"Try me." He's sort of sweaty and bulging and it's freaking me out.

So I hurry past him. "I'm sorry but I'm meeting someone and I'm late. It was nice talking to you."

"You and me should get together sometime," he says.

That's not going to happen in this lifetime or the next twelve, I don't bother saying. I keep walking, hoping I'm heading in the right direction.

"I'll look out for you," the jock calls after me.

Luckily, unless he likes to hang out in hidden corners of the library, he'll never find me.

My dorm isn't far. It's full of people carrying boxes and saying goodbye to their parents. A pang of something that's not quite sadness and not quite jealousy flutters, but I let it go. It doesn't matter anymore, that I'm alone. These people are starting their new lives, too, just like I am. Some are already partying. I slide past them and make my way up to the third floor.

My roommate is there, sitting on the bed next to the window that has a view out over the green. She's going through an open suitcase and she looks up when I walk in. She has long hair the color of polished copper and a sprinkling of freckles across her nose. Her face lights up, like she's genuinely happy to see me. "Hey, roomie. I'm Violet."

I smile back at her. It's impossible not to. She's fun, and nice, you just get that impression. "Millie."

"Hi, Millie. I hope you don't mind me claiming the bed next to the window," she says. "And the bigger closet. Your desk is bigger, though. And you have an extra bookshelf."

"No, that's fine."

"I saw you talking to that football player and his groupies," she says.

"You saw that?"

"I was feeling your pain." She laughs. "Those girls' faces when they saw it was *you* and not them he was chasing after."

"Well, they can have him. I hope I haven't already made a few enemies."

"Those girls will be fine as long as you stay away from the football team."

"You know them?"

"I know their type." She sets a picture of her family on her bedside table. She has a lot of brothers, it looks like. "My brother was the quarterback at my high school in Wilmington. My other brother was a wide receiver. And my *other* brother was a halfback. We had girls like that camping out on our doorstep every night of the week."

"Wow. Well, I'll definitely be staying away from the football team," I assure her. "As far away as possible."

"There's no way we're not going to the game tonight, though," Violet says. "You *have* to come with me. I don't know anyone else here yet."

I laugh a little as I put my bag on my bed and start unpacking it. "I'm probably going to skip the game, sorry."

"No *way*, roomie, you can't bail on me! I refuse to sit there by myself and I can't miss the opening game of the season. My brothers would kill me."

"I'm not really into football," I admit. I've honestly never watched much of it and couldn't tell you the rules if my life depended on it.

"What *are* you into?" Violet's face is open and sunny, like she's actually interested and not just asking to make small talk. So I find myself telling her.

"I'm a writer."

"That's so cool! Are you an English major?"

"Yeah. How about you?"

"Psychology. I'm planning on becoming a shrink. Believe it or not, it's been my lifelong ambition."

"Wow." I start putting some of my stuff into drawers.

"Yeah, just be careful. I might go all Freudian and start psycho-analyzing you any minute."

I smile without meaning to and it feels good. It's been a long time since I made a new friend. "I'll watch out for that."

"If you ever feel like you might need some therapy, just let me know. You can be my first patient."

I take my hat off and toss it onto my bed. My hair tumbles out and hangs past my shoulders. It's been a while since I cut it.

"Wow," she says. "Is that your real hair?"

I have strange hair. It's a very pale shade of red that's almost blond, but not quite. It looks pink under certain lights. A lot of people comment on it or stare at it or want to touch it, which is why I usually keep it hidden. I cut it shorter after my mother died, in one of those weird moments where you do something and you don't know why. But it's grown back since then. I have bangs and it's sort of angled around my face, unevenly in places, because going to a hairdresser wasn't something I could ever afford. "I'm thinking about dyeing it black."

"Don't you dare. It's amazing."

"So's yours." It really is. It's a coppery red with gold highlights.

Her phone pings and she's busy for a few seconds. Then she says, "So, what do you say? Kick-off is at four thirty."

"I don't know the first thing about football," I tell her.

"I'll teach you," she says. "Who knows, you might actually enjoy it."

Chapter Two

I climb out of the pool after doing my daily two hundred laps and grab a towel. My house, as usual, is quiet. It's been a long summer. I was glad to start football practice again, just to get out of my own fucking head. I have plenty of friends, but a lot of them go back to their hometowns for the summers, to hang out with their families. This *is* my hometown. And the only family I have left is a brother who was deployed to

Afghanistan eleven months ago and has been through some very real shit, and another brother who lives in Chicago. Besides, Gage is busy. He's basically the biggest manwhore on the planet, so even though we get along well, I always feel like I'm encroaching on his bed-hopping schedule.

Me ... well, I have the opposite problem.

Not that I couldn't bed hop if I wanted to. Not at all.

I don't, though. For ... reasons.

Reasons I prefer not to dwell on.

In fact, the whole topic is one I avoid like the plague.

The problem is, a lot of *other* people seem to thrive on speculating continuously, like they have nothing better to fucking do.

Maybe because I'm the starting quarterback. I'm 6'4" and I work out for four hours a day, so I'm built as fuck. I keep to myself when I'm not partying with friends or at practice, so I've been labeled "brooding" and "mysterious." Go figure.

The more I deflect, the more they want me.

Like now, as I park my car and make my way toward the players' entrance of the stadium.

"Hi, Bo."

I turn. It's three girls, hanging out next to a yellow Jeep. They've been waiting for me.

I glance at them as I walk past. "Hey."

"What are you doing for the next twenty minutes?" one of them asks.

"Getting ready to play a game of football."

"The game doesn't start for two hours," one points out.

I don't feel like having a conversation with these girls. They're dressed like they should be hanging out on a street corner. I wouldn't be surprised if they just finished banging the entire basketball team. *Be nice.* "We have warm up."

"What about later?" says the blond. "What are you doing after the game?"

"Celebrating, hopefully."

"We could meet up with you. That is, if you're sure you don't want us to help you warm up a little ... *before* warm up."

"Yeah, Bo," says the dark-haired one. "We could *all* help you warm up."

I keep walking. "Maybe another time."

My behavior would probably be considered strange to most people, I know that. Most guys would be thanking their lucky stars that every woman they meet is desperate for some goddamn action. My problem is, I can't bring myself to go with it.

Which could have something to do with the fact that my mother died of a particular aggressive form of pancreatic cancer on my fifteenth birthday. A few weeks later, my father hung himself in our garage. He loved her so much he just didn't want to live without her. On her death bed, my mother's final words to me were ... *promise me you'll stay true to your own heart.*

I told her I would.

Which I now regret.

Caleb joined the Marines a few years later and Gage coped by jumping into bed with legions of women, maybe for some kind of comfort or distraction, who knows. As for me, I'm stuck in a zone that's partly about honoring a promise and partly about trying to find a way to respect what my dead parents once had.

I'm not exactly fucking thrilled about any of it, but it's the hand I've been dealt: I'm incapable of letting myself have random, meaningless sex. I'm waiting for the real thing, as ludicrous as that might be.

And, since I've never met anyone who I could potentially see myself falling in love with—not even close—I've been saving myself for some elusive, perfect woman who might not even exist.

Who probably *doesn't* exist, let's be honest.

Which fucking sucks.

I *wish* I could climb into that Jeep and go for a joyride with these girls. I wish I could let off some metaphorical steam all over them. Take out my frustrations in a long-overdue frenzy until they were crying for more than one reason.

But no. I spend every single second of my time mired in a ferocious, feral state of relentless, raging lust. For a phantom lover who never shows up.

I exist in a haze of blazing, pent-up need that has nowhere to focus besides football, which only releases a minuscule fraction of it.

I hang out with friends, I swim until my muscles are aching, I pump iron until I'm drenched in sweat. But none of it helps.

It's a big fucking problem.

I'm glad the football season officially starts tonight. Now that I can immerse myself in practice, games and my business and finance classes, time won't seem so slow and heavy, I can only hope. Caleb will be home next month. My brother has seen some serious combat in Afghanistan and I have a feeling he'll be a changed man when he gets back. I email him every couple of days to try to boost his morale, which hasn't been great lately. It'll be good to have him home again.

The girls call after me, begging me to come back to them.

I almost turn.

I almost fucking do it.

Promise me ... stay true to your own heart.

I am. I said I would. But what if it kills me?

There's more to me than a heart. And everything else about me wants to fuck like a maniac.

I keep walking.

I get to the locker room and toss my bag onto a bench.

Most of the team is already there and we go through our plays and warm up and I do what I need to do. I try to focus.

Each day, it's getting harder.

My head isn't straight. My situation is starting to fuck with my concentration. I'm consumed with a raging fever that's becoming harder and harder to control.

As we run out onto the field for kick-off, I can hear the fans chanting my name. We're playing one of our biggest rivals tonight and they'll give us a run for our money, but I'm more than fucking up to it. I can feel the adrenaline pumping through my veins like a drug. The thrill of the game is the only thing that takes the slightest edge off.

I throw the ball to Kirby, who advances twelve yards. It's a good start. The fans go wild. It's our first game of the season and they're feeling it.

I nail pass after pass. By the end of the first half, we're up by fourteen points.

It's deep in the fourth quarter when it happens. Our possession. The score is 38-7. I'm getting into position for the next play when something catches my eye. I glance up at the Jumbotron.

And I stop.

The camera has zoomed in on someone. At first I think I'm seeing things. Imagining some kind of vision, dug up, maybe, by an agony that's only compounding itself day by day.

It's a girl. An unbelievably ... *beautiful* girl.

Her face is angelic, impossibly cute, like something out of ... a fantasy, maybe. A fantasy I want to step into and live inside. She's wearing a hat but as I stand there watching her, a gust of wind blows her hat off and her long hair spills loose. Her hair isn't quite strawberry blond and isn't quite white gold but some impossible shade in between, framing her face like a halo. The setting sun catches it. Everything about her shines with a surreal glow. She looks soft and enchanting and somehow shimmery, like a shy mermaid that just wandered onto dry land. You can tell she doesn't know the camera is on her. She smiles sort of self-consciously at something someone next to her has said and reaches for her hat.

Fuck, she's stunning. She's devastatingly sexy in a dreamy, totally-unaware-of-it way. *Jesus. I'm getting hard.* From gazing up at the fucking Jumbotron. Which is not ideal in the middle of a football game.

Someone's yelling at me. A *lot* of people are yelling at me. I can hear their voices, but I literally can't pull my eyes away.

I'm star-struck, like one of those shots in a movie where everything fades out except the object that takes all your focus. My mouth feels parched. And my heart aches as though I've been missing something monumental and here it suddenly fucking is.

Who is she?

I don't even realize I've said it out loud, but Tyler is within earshot. "That's the girl I saw on the green today. She's a fuckin' goddess."

I feel like lunging at him. Tackling him to the ground and making sure he understands that he can't have her. That if he goes anywhere near her, I'll go fucking ballistic.

But then she realizes she's on camera and her cheeks get pink as she puts her hat back on and pulls it low over her eyes.

The camera pans away, across the crowd, and she's gone.

No.

I scan the stadium but have no idea where she might be.

Coach is yelling from the sideline. He calls a time out. His face is bright red. Hayes and Kowalski and some of the others are laughing. I realize I've been standing there for a while, maybe close to a minute.

"McCabe! What the hell are you doing?" Coach is screaming.

"He's checking out some girl on the Jumbotron," Kirby says. He elbows me. "Does this mean our lone wolf quarterback has finally met his match? Dude, you need to find her."

34

I know.

My team gives me shit all the time about my lack of a love life. They don't understand it and neither do I.

Coach is about a foot shorter than me, ranting like a lunatic. He's worked up. "If you have any intention of continuing as the starting goddamn quarterback for this team, McCabe, you'll get your goddamn head back in this game, and pronto! You can play the other field in your own time. Is that understood?"

"Yes, sir."

I scan the crowd as subtly as I'm capable of as I return to the field. I can't see her.

Fuck.

It takes every shred of willpower I possess to keep my focus. Somehow, I do. For the final fifteen minutes, I go through the motions. Bronson's a wild card with occasional flashes of genius. And he's right where I want him. My pass glides into his outstretched hands and he juggles it before securing the ball.

Touchdown! yells the announcer. The crowd goes insane.

The game is over.

I have to stop myself from running up into the stands to search for her. But there are a hundred thousand people here tonight. They're standing up. They're starting to leave.

Where is she?

Who is she?

I have to find out.

I want to see her again, *like I've never wanted anything in my life.*

The people around me are cheering, celebrating, patting me on the back. I barely hear them. All I can think about is the shy, glowing girl and the realization that's hitting me like a ten-ton wall of bricks.

I'm going to search for her until I find her. If it takes me the rest of my life to do it.

I've kept my promise, and now it's time to find out what I've been missing.

To make the most beautiful girl I've ever seen …

mine.

I want *her.*

Chapter Three

Millie

Violet and I take our seats in the stands. This place is huge. And packed.

We drink our cokes and Violet's right, this is actually kind of fun. Everyone in the stadium is buzzing. They all start chanting and waving their banners and stomping their feet when our team runs out onto the field. Violet chants along with everyone else.

We want Bo. We want Bo. We want Bo.

I can't help but ask her the obvious, once the cheers have died down a little. "Who's Bo?"

She laughs. "Seriously?" She seems to find my total ignorance hilarious. She's such a football fan she actually reads about these players in her spare time and follows the scores and the schedules and their social media accounts and whatnot.

"I told you, I'm not really that into football."

"Bo McCabe is only one of the hottest quarterbacks in the country, and not just in the good-at-football kind of way, Millie. Jeez. But it's a well-known fact that he doesn't date. At all. People are saying that he's saving himself for his one true love. Can you *believe* that?"

"Wow."

"Of course every girl swoons over him not only because he's a romantic but also because he's freaking gorgeous. I mean, *look* at that guy, would you?"

"It's kind of hard to tell with the helmet on."

"Here. I'll show you." Violet pulls her phone out of her pocket and googles him.

She brings up a photo and I stare at him for a few seconds. He's tall and has mink-brown hair that's messed up and sweaty. He's holding his helmet under his very-muscular arm. He's smiling at the camera, his other arm slung around the shoulders of one of his teammates. His handsomeness has a rugged edge to it. There's a wild look to him, like he'd be ... *a lot to handle. And outrageously good at ... everything.*

Millie, what?

I don't even know why that particular thought enters my head. I don't usually think about things like that. I'm usually too distracted.

This Bo McCabe is beautiful and all-American and masculine as hell. And yes, I can admit he's gorgeous. One of those people who won the good looks lottery.

It hardly matters. I hand Violet's phone back. I have bigger things to worry about than how good-looking the quarterback is. *Or* whether or not he sleeps around. I have a book to write, and I'm feeling sort of guilty that I'm not working on it right now.

But the game is entertaining to watch. Bo McCabe is very good, even I can see that. He seems level-headed. He's coolly thinking about what he's doing, measuring up his decisions. Every single time, he throws the ball right into the hands of his receiver with a precision that's mesmerizing. Our team scores four touchdowns and each time, the stadium erupts.

I'm surprised to find myself just as engrossed in this game as Violet is. Silently, I'm cheering for him. I want him to get the glory he deserves. His nerves of steel and his crazy accuracy are winning this game. He's making it easy for the rest of them.

"He's *really* good," I comment vaguely. The wind has picked up and my hat gets blown off.

Violet glances over at me, laughing. She has one of those proverbial twinkles in her eye. "Admit it, you're as smitten as every other female with a heartbeat."

I can't help smiling back at her but I don't bother answering. It hardly matters either way. I reach for my hat and put it back on. "I think he's good at *football*, that's all I said."

"Wait, what's he doing?" Violet says. "Why's he just standing there?"

I look at what she's pointing to. It's Bo. He's standing in the middle of the field, watching the huge TV screen. The sun is low and is shining on the screen from this angle, so I can't clearly see what he's staring at.

"Millie!" gasps Violet. "It's you! You're on the Jumbotron! Wave!"

"What?"

"Oh, it moved," she says. "But you were on there!"

God. How mortifying.

Bo McCabe is still standing in the middle of the field. Now he's scanning the crowd, like he's looking for someone. People are murmuring. His coach is yelling and making irate hand gestures. Their team has called a time out.

Violet turns to me. "Millie, holy shit. He was looking at *you* on the big screen. He stopped playing to stare at *you.*"

"No." I laugh lightly. "That's ridiculous."

"He *was.*"

Some of the people in the stands nearby are turning.

To stare.

At me.

They're pointing at me. One of them takes a picture.

Shit.

I pull my hat lower.

I really hate it when people stare at me. It makes me feel panicky. I didn't like being stared at as I was walking through the trailer park, and I don't like it now. If there's one thing I loathe, it's any kind of limelight.

And I've had enough. "I'm going back to the dorm, Violet. The game's almost over anyway. I really do need to get some work done."

Violet seems to be tuning into the fact that I'm practically on the verge of a panic attack. I feel spooked. *Why are all those people looking at me? Because of what Violet said? They think the quarterback stopped playing to stare at* me? It doesn't make any sense.

The thought makes my stomach do a funny little flip, like I've just hit the summit of a roller coaster. I can practically feel the gravity-defying g-forces that are way more intense than I could ever handle.

"I need to leave."

"I'll come with you," Violet says, linking her arm through mine. Her offer somehow locks this friendship into place. She *gets* something about how I'm feeling right now and she's here for me, is what she's saying. "We'll beat the rush. Come on."

We stand up and make our way down the stairs. I pull the collar of my jacket up and my hat is as low as it can go without actually covering my eyes. Once we're away from the stands, I start to feel a little better.

Another cheer erupts behind us. They must have scored again.

I find myself feeling sort of ... glad. For Bo. He'll be the hero of the day and he deserves it.

And I'm even more glad to be *out of there*. I'm not good at crowds.

From now on, I'll stick to my quiet corners of the library and keep to myself. The very last thing I need is to be pointed at and broadcast over a giant Jumbotron.

Chapter Four

"You pull a stunt like that again, McCabe, and you'll find yourself sitting on the goddamn bench for the rest of the season." We're back in the locker room and Coach is still ranting. I tune it out. I say what I need to say to placate him, because it makes sense to downplay this as much as possible. *It won't happen again, Coach.* But it's all bullshit. He wouldn't bench me even if hell froze over. I'm the guy every NFL team is salivating over and a big part of the reason our stadium is packed every game, we both know that.

Besides, I'm too distracted to give any answer that requires too much thought.

I'll start by searching the dorms, the cafeterias, the bars. Does she go here? Is she a freshman? A transfer? A local?

I've lived in this town my whole life. Both my brothers played football here and I've been a student at this university for three years. I'd have seen her. She must be new.

Maybe she's in the parking lot, walking to her car.

I'm about to run out and check when Tyler slings his arm around my shoulders and Kirby takes a photo. I'm not smiling.

"I'm captioning this with *#WhoIsShe,* *#JumbotronAngel* and *#BoWantsToKnow,*" Kirby says.

"Someone find that clip from the Jumbotron," Tyler adds.

"No," I tell Kirby, grabbing the front of his jersey with my fist. "Don't fucking post that." But it's true. Someone will have it. *And if someone has a photo of her, maybe I can find out who she is.*

My team is already on a mission, led by Shawn Kirby, who's obnoxious as fuck, even though, somewhere under all that loud-mouthed swagger, he's loyal and happens to be a good friend. He's a shit-hot flanker. He also has a massive Instagram following. Kirby's one of those people who thrives on showing off and telling everyone about the smallest details of his life.

I'm, on the other hand ... not.

Management likes us to use social media, since it's easy publicity. I've got just as many followers as Kirby, even though I've only posted the occasional photo of myself playing football.

Kirby posts everything, from what he ate for breakfast to the string of women he juggles daily to whatever protein drink he's advertising.

It's something I'll probably need to up my game with before draft picks start hotting up, even though I'm a million miles from the publicity whore status Kirby loves to bask in.

I reach for Kirby's phone but he yanks it away. "Too late, sunshine." He grins at me.

He pisses me off on an hourly basis, but this is taking it to another level. The last thing I need is Kirby messing with ... *this.* "What the fuck, Kirby? You *posted* that?"

"If this girl can bring our star quarterback—whose mood happens to be atrocious and we all know why—to a gaga standstill in the middle of the opening game, then we need to know who she is."

"*I'll* find out who she is. You stay the fuck out of it."

"Sorry, man," he says. "It's just been transmitted worldwide."

I take a swing at him but he ducks, the little fucker.

Tyler's sitting on one of the benches, scrolling on his phone. "Kirby, you're getting comments. Shit, look at this. Someone found the video."

I release Kirby and grab Tyler's phone. They gather around me but everything fades out as soon as I see it.

Someone posted the clip.

Of her.

My heart feels like it's trying to hotly throb its way right the fuck out of my chest.

Holy fucking hell.

The cameraperson zoomed right in and lingered on her much longer than they usually would. And no wonder.

Her face.

That shy smile.

The glow of her outrageous hair.

I can even see what color her eyes are. Pale, silver-gray with darker rims. Like bottled lightning.

"Wow," I hear myself say. I sit down on the bench, holding her image carefully in my hands.

Someone pats my shoulder, like they're tuning in to whatever's happening to me. I'm only vaguely aware of the things my teammates are saying.

"Don't worry, man. We'll find her."

"I'm sure it was her on the green today, Bo. She must go here."

The next comment splices straight through the haze: "Bo. Look at this. It's on this guy's Snapchat story. *Served her today at the coffee truck. Order: hot chocolate. Gave her two extra marshmallows #JumbotronAngel.*"

I stand up and look at Hayes's phone. The handle is @masonsjava. "Hayes, do you know this guy?"

"Yeah, he runs the coffee truck. I've been to a couple of parties at his house."

Replies start popping up. Two. Five. Ten. Twenty.

Shit.

This whole thing is going viral.

Because of me.

The realization does something strange to me. My heartbeat is hot but the rest of me goes cold.

People will be searching for her.

A lot of people.

I need to get to her first.

I need to shield her.

I need to make sure no one goes near her.

I have to stop myself from grabbing the front of Hayes's shirt in my fist and doing something reckless. Like punching him in the face. "Message him. Ask him if he knows who she is or where she lives."

"Bo. Someone posted another photo," says Kowalski. "In the stands, leaving with a friend. Before the game even ends, it looks like."

Kowalski shows me the photo. She has her hat pulled down low and the collar of her jacket turned up. She clearly doesn't want to be seen. Other people in the stands are staring at her.

I've done this to her.

And now I can't undo it.

Hayes has a reply. "Mason doesn't know where she lives. He gave her his number and invited her to a party tonight but she hasn't called him. She's a freshman, she told him. Her name is Millie."

Millie.

If she has a name, then she must be real. This whole thing is fucking with my mind.

She's real.

"So she'll be in one of the freshman dorms," says Kirby. "There can't be that many of them. How many freshmen go to this school?"

Tyler's googling it. "Around seven thousand. Eighteen dorms house freshmen."

"You saw her on the green," I murmur.

"Yeah. She said she was meeting someone at her dorm. She was holding the campus map. So it's probably nearby."

"We're going to find her." I'm the orchestrator, the signal caller, the play maker, the game manager. And right now, I need my team. "Don't scare her or stalk her or chase her or freak her out in any way whatsoever. She's mine." I regret saying that last line out loud.

"Sure, Bo," says Tyler. "We get it."

Tyler high-fives Kirby. I glare at them.

"What?" Kirby grins. "We're just happy for you, man."

Kowalski says what I'm thinking. "You realize this is totally fucking crazy, right, Bo? You saw her for ten seconds on the Jumbotron and now, suddenly, she's the one you've been waiting for all this time? Do you know how insane that sounds? She'll think you're a fucking lunatic."

"I know that. I never said she's the one." *Even though I have this feeling she is the one.*

Either way, he's right. This is totally fucked up.

I don't care.

I just want to meet her.

I want to see her face again.

In person.

For real.

Because I feel like I've been sacked by a linebacker when I wasn't expecting it, while simultaneously having my heart ripped out of my chest and my brain hijacked by a lightning-eyed vision that has taken over every thought and every desire.

"I just want to make sure she's okay. I don't want her getting harassed."

And then I want to talk to her and stare at her and bask in her glow.

Before I lose my mind for a hundred different reasons.

Chapter Five

Millie

We get back to the dorm and it's practically empty because everyone's still at the game.

"I'm going over to the library for a few hours," I tell Violet.

"I'm just going to chill here and listen to some music. I'll probably have an early night."

"I'll try to not wake you when I get back."

She's sitting on her bed, scrolling on her phone. "I still can't believe Bo McCabe was watching you on the Jumbotron."

"I'm sure he wasn't. He was probably just blinded by the glare or something."

"Oh, look, they've scored another touchdown in the final minute."

"Sorry I made you leave early, Violet."

"Don't worry about it. You can make it up to me when we go to the next game. It's finished now, anyway."

I don't mention that I'm probably done going to football games. Five minutes of Jumbotron fame is five too many. "See you later."

"Good luck with the writing."

I close the door and make my way downstairs. I walk over to the library, which is lit up and inviting. I pass two girls, who glance at me, more curiously than maybe they should. I pull my hat lower. I take the elevator up to the top floor of the library and look for a place to work. In the far corner of the room, there's a quiet, empty study corner with desks and a couch, a couple of beanbags and even a comfortable-looking window seat. It's perfect.

I sit in the window seat.

I open my laptop and find the document I'm looking for. My second novel. My first book was a sort-of fictionalized version of my life so far. It's a harrowing story, so it got people's attention. It'll be in bookstores in just over a month, which is both exciting and daunting. It's a strange thing to do, laying out your innermost thoughts and the most intense kind of pain you've ever felt, for other people to judge in whatever way they will. But it felt good to let it spool out onto the pages, like a kind of therapy.

Anyway, it's nice to have time to concentrate, after the whirlwind of the past few weeks, of getting ready to leave my life behind. God knows I was more than ready. The packing up. The saying goodbye to people I'll probably never see again. The long bus trip. The sights. The whole new world.

That's what I've decided to write about. The possibilities. The invisible just-out-of-reach glimmer that you may or may not end up reaching.

But before I even finish my first sentence, my phone starts ringing.

Who would be calling me?

Violet flashes up on the screen. We exchanged numbers at the football game.

"Hey, roomie," I answer. "What's up?"

"Millie. Don't freak out, okay?"

"Why would I? What's going on?"

"One of the football players, whose name is Shawn Kirby—he's the one that caught the pass for the second touchdown, remember?"

"Um, I guess so."

"Well, he posted a photo of Bo right after the game and holy shit they're looking for you."

"What?"

"They're calling you the 'Jumbotron Angel' and, well, you've sort of … gone viral."

"Gone … *viral?*" I whisper.

"The clip. Of you. And the hashtags. It's … Bo Wants To Know."

"Bo wants to know what?"

"Who you are. They figured out what your name is because of some coffee truck guy and now the whole team and possibly the entire campus is trying to find you."

What? *Oh my God.*

This is not good. Panic prickles behind my brain. I don't like being searched for. Thought about. Singled out. It's … just a hang-up I have, after all the things I've been through.

I try to do what I always do when I feel scared. I take a deep breath. I count to seven, for some reason. If I believed in lucky numbers, it's the one I'd choose.

"Are you okay, Millie?"

"They won't find me. I'm in a very hidden corner and it's completely deserted up here."

"Do you want me to come over there? So you're not alone?"

"Thank you, Violet. But no. I'll be fine. I'll lay low for a couple of hours. By then I'm sure whatever's going on will have died down. I hope. I'll see you later on."

"Millie?"

"Yeah?"

"If they do end up finding you ... I hear he's a nice guy once you get to know him. He's not a stuck-up jerk, like some quarterbacks. He's never done anything like this before."

She's telling me to give him a chance, in other words.

I don't know how to tell Violet that my life happened in a way that turned me inwards instead of out. I saw that photo of her family, her smiling mother who probably told her on a daily basis how much she loved her. Her stable father and strapping older brothers who'd do anything to protect her and keep her safe. Those things just didn't happen in my case. I don't wallow in it and at this point it's all just water under the bridge, but for better or worse, those details have shaped my personality. I've felt alone and vulnerable for a long time. So I hide. Especially when it comes to men. I don't look at them. I don't talk to them. I keep to myself. It's the only way I know how to protect myself. It provides a forcefield that gives me at least the illusion of safety.

And now some bigshot quarterback thinks he has some sort of *claim* on me just because he saw me on a big screen TV? And everyone thinks he's so deserving and special because he's hot and also not a manwhore?

I don't think so.

I'm so focused all the time on *not* letting my guard down that I don't even know *how* to let my guard down, and especially not with someone like Bo McCabe, who's successful and gorgeous and dripping with luck. I've been forced by self-preservation to become a freakish, socially-stunted hermit. The only thing I know how to *do* is to keep to myself.

It's a hard thing to try to describe to my new roommate. "They won't find me," I say again.

She pauses, like she's not sure it'll work out the way I'm hoping it does. "If they show up here, what do you want me to say?"

"Tell them you've never heard of me and that they should go away."

Violet exhales a small laugh. "I doubt it's going to be that easy to brush them off, but I'll do my best. Call me if anything happens, okay?"

"I will. Thanks. I'm glad you're my roomie, Violet."

"Me too, Millz."

It's been a while since I've connected to anyone in such a real way.

We end the call and I look around. There's no one else here. It's quiet. The coast is clear. So I turn back to my laptop.

A memory drifts, of scattered needles on a dingy carpet. Her cold hand. But then my thoughts slide past all that, as I've trained them to do. All the way to a neon green field. A football is flying straight toward me in its perfect, steady, spiraling arc. For some reason, in my daydream, I catch it.

I'm stunned out of my own head when one of the two elevators pings from the far end of the large, segmented room. All the bookshelves are lower up here, so you can see over them. Which affords me a view of two very large, very muscular men walking out of the elevator. It's not hard to tell they're football players, partly because they're enormous. They're breathing heavily, like they've been running.

Oh, shit.

Instinctively, I curl further back into my window seat.

But they've already seen me.

Shit shit shit! They're walking over to me.

I don't know who they are, but I know they're not Bo.

Would it matter if they were?

"Those girls were right," one of them says. *Damn it.* It must have been the girls who stared at me as I was walking into the library. If I'd known people were looking for me or that there were scouts all over campus, I would have worn a better disguise.

The two football players approach me and stand close to the window seat, sort of hulking over me. I'm clutching my laptop like it's a shield. But they don't actually look threatening, aside from the sheer size of them. They look sort of ... friendly. This does little to tone down my unease.

"It *is* you," one of them says. "You're the Jumbotron Angel."

Who came up with *that* one, I'm wondering.

"Are you Millie?" asks the other one.

What to say? I don't want to be ... *viral.* Can I slide past them and disappear? Probably not. So I decide to be straight up with them. "Yes. But I'm not interested in being stalked, by you or anyone else. So if you wouldn't mind leaving me alone, that would be fantastic. You have a good night now," I add, trying to gently dismiss them.

But one of them is taking out his phone. Pushing a call button. "Bo? We found her. Yeah. In the library. Top floor."

Wow.

To be honest, being stalked isn't a particularly new thing for me. I've spent most of my life in three different trailer parks in low-rent areas of mid Florida. If you want to find strange, out-there men with stalkerish tendencies, I can tell you it's a hotbed of exactly that type of person.

But this is taking stalking to a whole new level. I'm being stalked by an entire football team. And I'm not entirely sure why. Plus, I have a deadline.

I close my laptop and slide it into my bag. "Look, I didn't ask for this. So if you'll excuse me, I'm leaving. I'll go find another place to work."

They don't move. They just stand there, like a wall of built, pumped-up muscle.

I glare up at them.

One of them has a big grin on his face. He's blinking at me. "We're harmless, by the way. We just wanted to make sure we got to you first. So you don't get harassed."

I feel compelled to point out the obvious. "What you're doing ... *is* sort of harassment. Just saying."

"Trust me, you'll need us if the mob shows up. The news is already out that you're in the library."

Shit.

Social media has a lot to answer for.

They're both still staring at me.

"Wow," the slightly shorter one says, which isn't saying much, since the other one is probably 6'5" or something.

"Yes, *wow* is exactly what I was thinking, too." I'm trying not to be rude, but it's been an intense day. "That you would think this is acceptable, tracking me down like this. Now if you could please move aside, I'm leaving."

It doesn't seem like they've heard me. And they're not showing even an inkling of remorse. Still grinning. "My name's Shawn. This is Tyler. We're friends of Bo's."

Like that should make a difference to me. "I've never met Bo," is what they seem to be forgetting.

"Oh, you'll love Bo. He's basically the best person I know, in pretty much every conceivable category."

"Yeah," says the yeti-like one named Tyler. Come to think of it, he looks familiar. I realize it's the same guy who spoke to me on the green earlier today. "Bo's cool," he says.

Cool?

"He's got this dedication to his teammates and his brothers that goes above and beyond, and I'm not just saying that. You can't help but respect the hell out of the guy."

I'm not sure why they're telling me all this, but for some reason it takes the edge off my annoyance. They don't seem like bad people. They seem earnest and enthusiastic about their mission.

"Well, as nice as it is to meet you both, I'm not sure what any of this is even about so if you could please move out of my way, I really do have things I need to get started on."

"Bo would kill us if we let you leave," Tyler says.

Shawn glances over at Tyler. "Bo would kill us if we *didn't* let her do whatever the hell she wants to do."

Tyler contemplates this for a second. "You're right."

"Luckily for all of us," I point out, "it's not up to Bo to *let* me do anything."

The elevator pings again and we all glance over at it.

At least ten people pour out of the elevator in a loud, boisterous rush. They're clearly hunting for someone. I guess we all know who that someone is. "It's her!" a girl shrieks, pointing at me. Some are taking out their phones.

Oh no.

"I don't want my photo taken," I tell them, sliding deeper back into the window seat. This is actually kind of terrifying. There's a sting behind my eyes.

I'm trapped.

"Hey," Shawn says, noticing my anxiety. "Don't worry about a thing, Millie. That's what we're here for." He elbows Tyler.

Tyler folds his arms and turns to face the crowd. "Consider us your defensive line. Nothing's getting through us, Millie."

Shawn yells at the crowd. "No photos unless you want Tyler here tackling you and confiscating your goddamn phone. Go home. It's over. Go on. Out. *Out.*"

"Does Bo know you've found her?" some guy asks.

Before anyone can answer him, the other elevator pings and slides open. A few people gasp and squeal, which makes me wonder what's happening. I peek through the small gap between my two bodyguards.

"It's Bo!" someone hollers.

"Oh my God, he's so freaking hot," a girl gushes.

"Hi, Bo."

"Can I get your autograph, Bo?"

"Good game tonight, Bo," a guy says. "You were amazing."

Then I hear another voice. It's deep and commanding and has a husk to it. Let me guess. "This whole thing has gotten way out of hand. Go back to your rooms. There's nothing to see here. My boys here will take your names and we'll make sure that each one of you gets a ticket to the next game if you agree to leave right now. Are we clear?" Even his voice is perfect.

"Sure, Bo," someone says. Like their leader has spoken and they'll take his word as gospel. "We'll leave you and Millie to talk."

Wow. My life has become a reality show.

And my heart's beating fast.

Bo is here.

I'm not sure why that means something, but after all this, it does. His presence in this room is infusing everything with a sense of calmness and control. Bo McCabe is one of those people that inspires people to follow him, you can *feel* that.

Shawn leans closer to me and says, "Don't be afraid of him. He'll do absolutely anything you say." Then the two of them walk over to the small crowd, who gather around them.

I lean back against the wall of my window seat, wishing like hell I could somehow time warp into a parallel universe.

The crowd are being moved into the elevator. Shawn and Tyler get in with them. I hear the glide of the elevator doors closing. And, suddenly, the room is very quiet again.

Someone—an extremely *large* someone whose strapping, electric presence is filling up the room—comes over and leans his shoulder against the wall next to the window seat, his arms folded.

Mr. Star Quarterback, of course.

I look up at him. Up this close he's … well, he's stunning. His mink-brown hair is unruly and has a wave to it, curling at the ears. He's *huge*, which is emphasized by his football padding. He might be as tall as 6'4". He's got one of those bodies that's long and lean but at the same time muscled and toned, like a sculpture come to life. Sparkling blue eyes are staring straight at me. It's a color movie stars get cast for, for that reason alone.

He's ridiculously handsome. His eyes glow with a fever that's intense enough to ... well, I don't know *what* they're intense enough to do. Definitely *something*.

His face breaks into a smile, which, weirdly, almost makes me return the smile. It's just so genuine. There's something relieved about it.

He's something to be marveled at, no doubt about it.

Someone *else* can do the marveling.

"I'm sorry about all this," he says. "Kirby posted before I could stop him."

He pulls up a chair and sits, knees apart. He doesn't seem to care that I don't *want* him to sit next to me. Or that I can't think of a single thing to say to him.

He's gorgeous, he's the starting quarterback, and he's filling out that football outfit like nobody's business. A girl would have to be made of stone not to notice. And those blue eyes framed by dark lashes really are kind of spectacular. His smile is basically lighting up the room.

I can hardly bear the heat of his gaze. He's staring at me like he's happy to see me. *Very* happy. And I have no idea why he would be.

He's not helping my situation by being so damn *built* and beautiful and fascinated as he watches me watch him. He folds his buff arms across his chest and contemplates me. Then he smiles again.

"I'm Bo," he finally says. "Bo McCabe." His voice is deep and has a husky layer to it. He leans forward and offers his hand.

I hesitate before taking it. His grip is warm and strong and ... *oh, hell, this is too much* ... is making me *very* aware of the smoldering current of heat that's radiating from him. He turns my hand and places a very light kiss on the back of it before I slide it away. "I know."

"You're Millie." I'll admit I like the way he says my name. There's something soft and endearing about the way he handles the word.

"Yes."

"Don't be scared of me."

"I'm not scared."

I glare at him. The thing is, I *am* scared of him. I know that if I let this god-like football hero into my life, he'll ruin it. He'd tell me I'm special, like he's about to do. That he saw me in a crowd and liked the color of my hair, or something. Then he'll proceed to break me in a thousand ways. Ways I've been broken before and still haven't healed from. And new ways, too. Ways that involve firsts and feelings and fatal mistakes. I can just tell.

"You're a freshman."

"Yes."

"You arrived today."

"It sounds like you pretty much know everything there is to know about me. So I guess we're done here."

He's watching me with this rapt, almost-amused look on his face. "Actually," he says, "I think we're just getting started."

I can't handle anything to do with this football hero. Not now. Maybe not ever.

After weathering the storms of the things that have happened to me, I'm wary now. I need my heart and my head intact if I'm going to finish my book, which I'll have to do to afford the rest of my tuition and graduate from college so I can be more than a trailer trash junkie, like my doomed mother.

"Listen. Bo. You seem nice, but I'm not sure why you're here and I don't really have a lot of time for a social life right now. You should go back to your football friends. I know you have a lot to celebrate."

"I don't want to go back to them," he says. "I want to talk to you."

It doesn't make any sense. "Why?"

"Why?" He blinks at me. He rubs his hand across his square jaw, like he's thinking about what to say. "I don't really know how to describe it without sounding like a complete lunatic."

"Try."

It's mildly entertaining, watching him fumble with this. He's so incredibly self-assured in every other way. "When I saw you on the Jumbotron, it was like all the light in the stadium landed on you. You quite literally lit up the entire goddamn *stadium*. I've never seen anyone do that before. I needed to find out who you were."

This makes me exhale a laugh without meaning to. "That's ... crazy."

"I know." He sounds almost pissed off about it. "But that's what happened. Then when I couldn't find you and I didn't know if I'd ever be able to see for myself if you were real or just some kind of, I don't know, *vision* ... I thought I might lose it."

"Lose what?"

He's thinking again. "My sanity," he says simply. "I wanted to see you again. Like I've never wanted anything in my life."

I think that might possibly be the nicest thing anyone has ever said to me.

But my emotional armor is far too fortified at this point to let an offhand compliment—if that's even what it was—to fully penetrate.

He's still talking. "And now that I *have* found you, and you're not a mirage, and you're even more dazzling in person than I could've ever dreamed up, I'm afraid you're stuck with me."

Wait. "Stuck with you?"

"Yes."

Even though the words he's saying are totally insane, there's a hopefulness in his expression that's sweet and intense. It makes an impression. It kind of leeches over into my airspace, touching my aura. And I'm not usually a person who thinks about *auras,* but that's what it feels like. Something about him is brushing up against something about me, and it's ... connective.

I meet his gaze for a few seconds, but the blue blaze of his eyes is too wild. It's like having a staring contest with a superhero.

He looks around, noticing the laptop sticking out of my bag. "Why are you studying on a Friday night? It's your first day of college. You should be out with your new friends. Classes don't even start until Monday."

I don't really want to lay it all out for him, but he's waiting for my reply. Very intently, like he's riveted by what I'm about to say. "I'm writing a book. I have a deadline."

"What kind of book?"

"A novel."

"What's it about?"

I sigh. "Look. Bo. I'm not talking to you about that. I don't talk about my books before I write them. I don't want to jinx them. And I have to go now."

"You can tell me about it when you've finished, then."

"Sure," I say, but it's an empty reply. It would imply that he and I will be having a conversation four months from now. Which has a snowball's chance in hell of happening. My sane mind has already convinced me to run a mile from this grade-A specimen of too much pumped-up masculinity to even think about handling.

My phone rings.

Violet flashes up on the screen. "It's my roommate."

Bo stands up, as though to give me some space. Even if it's only three feet. I watch him as he leans his shoulder against the wall again and folds his arms. *Wow*. He really is incredibly ... *buff*.

"Hey, roomie. What's up?"

"Millie! Oh my God, are you still at the library?"

"Yes."

"Well, don't come back here! I had to lock the door because there are, like, *a hundred* people here who are looking for you. Or more than that. They're banging on the door! They want to know if you're going to go on a date with Bo."

Our first names are on our dorm room doors.
"Shit."

"Millie, they're *crazy*."

Why is this happening? "Thanks for the heads-up."

"I'll call you back as soon as the coast is clear. For now, stay where you are, okay?"

"I will."

"I'll call you back."

Just as I'm ending the call, Shawn and Tyler burst through the door that comes from the fire exit staircase, making me jump. "Bo!" Shawn yells. "You and Millie have to get the fuck out of here! There's a mob down there! They're fucking rabid!"

Holy shit.

"Hurry!" Tyler's holding the door for us. "They're in the elevator."

We all glance over to the elevator. The light above the door says 3. We're on the fourth floor.

Bo grabs my backpack and slings it over his shoulder. Then he scoops me into his arms like I weigh nothing.

"Hey—"

"I'm faster," he says. Then he carries me through the door Tyler's holding, and down the stairs. I don't even protest. I'm too freaked out by what's going on.

They're all over campus? They're chasing us?

We reach the first floor and go out the back door of the library, following Tyler and Shawn to a monster truck of a blue pick-up that's waiting for us. Two football players are in the front seat, so by the time Tyler and Shawn get in to the back of the double cab, the only spot for me is on Bo's lap. He pulls me onto him as he climbs in. He's all powerful muscles and hard ridges and ... *oh, God.*

"I've got you," Bo says. "Everything's fine."

The words deflect off my forcefield. *I've got you? Everything's fine?*

Instead of being intimidated by him, which I *should* be, I feel almost comforted by how solid and strong he is. Which is *very* solid. *Very big, very hard and very ... close.* I'm sitting on top of him and his burly arms aren't just slung around me but wrapped around me. *And the enormous ridge I happen to be sitting directly on is ... oh, hell.*

How did I get here?

The moving colors of the night reflect off the windows as we drive through campus. There are people everywhere. I'm glad the truck's windows are tinted. But then I notice we're *leaving* campus. "Where are we going?"

"To my house."

"No. Bo, take me to my dorm. I want to go back to my room."

"You can't, Millie. It's not safe."

"It's true," says the gargantuan driver. "We've got a man stationed there and the place is swarming."

Bo's face, as I stare at him blurrily, because I'm scared and my eyes are leaking, is heart-breaking. I don't know why I say that, it just is.

I can't handle this.

But I guess I have to. I can't go back to my room or the library. Or anywhere else.

"Why do they even care about who I am?" I hear myself asking.

"Because I do," he says.

Chapter Six

Holy fuck.

She's wearing an oversized gray coat and a little black hat that, on anyone else, would look odd or completely nondescript. On her, it's the cutest fucking thing I've ever seen. If she's wearing any make-up, I can't tell. She cuts her own hair (the pink-gold pieces sticking out from under her cap are jagged and different lengths). Her eyes, up close, are an electric silver-gray, rimmed with charcoal, like a spooked little wolf. She has olive skin, a few freckles and her lips are the color of cotton candy. Her face is pixie-cute and stunningly gorgeous.

I'm trying not to stare.

I have to stop myself from carrying her away with me like a fucking caveman. But we're in Kowalski's truck on our way to my house. Which is good. It means I don't have to do anything crazy, at least not yet.

She's forced by circumstance to sit on my lap and let me hold her. Which is both the best thing that's ever happened to me and the absolute worst. It's fucking *agonizing*. Maybe she won't be able to tell that I'm harder than I've ever been in my life or that she happens to be sitting directly on top of approximately ten and a half inches of pure, feverish torture.

I want to devour her. I want to unzip her jacket so I can see more of her. I want to rip it off and wrap myself around her. To get closer. As close as it's possible to get.

I don't.

"Everything's okay," I say to her, but she's still shaken from the mob.

We pull up to the front gate of my house. There are a couple hundred people gathered around the front of my house, holding signs. *#Jumbotron Angel. #BoWantsToKnow, And So Do We! True Love Reigns.*

What the fuck is wrong with these people?

We drive through them and they part for us, trying to look in the windows, which are mostly opaque but not entirely.

Millie pulls her hat even lower over her eyes. People are yelling, taking pictures, cheering.

I unlock the gate with my phone app and Kowalski drives forward. He lowers his window and yells, "Stay the fuck out or we will pummel each and every one of you."

The threat works. The gates close behind us.

"This is your *house*?" Millie says, watching the thick iron gates slide closed.

"Yeah." My house is huge. It's made of stone and sits on seventeen acres. There's the main house, a lake house and a dock by a lake. There's a stone wall topped with a tall iron fence and security cameras running the entire length of the property. Why? Because my dad was *eccentric*, they used to call him. And rich as fuck. So he built what's basically a fortified castle. He had a knack for investing in businesses that hit major pay dirt, partly because he spent all his time studying the numbers. He had an IQ of somewhere around 145. It didn't save him though, from his one weakness: my mother.

So every dollar I've ever made, I've invested. My dad insisted my brothers and I learn that shit from a young age. He used to make it into a competition when we were kids. *Who can invest this fifty dollars and come out on top?* Like a game. Since all three of us are insanely competitive, we learned fast.

"Holy shit," she says.

Of course I'm wondering at this point if it's possible to fall in love this fast. Every single thing about her is my new favorite thing on the entire goddamn planet. From the light husk of her voice to the uneven cut of her hair to the way her palm is resting on my arm. *She's holding onto me as we drive.* Like an anchor.

My lust has gone into overdrive, but it's more than that. This lust has an edge. Of fascination. And of one-hundred-proof *possessiveness*. If anyone else so much as *looks* in her direction, I might do something mind-numbingly rash. Like beat them to an unrecognizable bloody pulp.

I hope no one tests me.

Kowalski drives us up to the front door of the house. "Thanks, man," I say. I don't invite them in and they pick up on whatever vibe I'm emitting because none of them suggest it, which is unusual. I have an indoor Olympic-sized pool and a killer games room with a pool table, pinball machines, a foosball table, a 72-inch TV and a fully stocked bar. It's our usual hang-out. Tonight, though, there's been a change of plans.

"You sure you don't want us to help you keep guard?" Kirby asks.

"No. It's fine. My security system is basically impenetrable."

"Just let us know if you need us for anything, Bo."

"Thanks for saving me from the paparazzi," Millie says to them.

They all turn to look at her and it's ludicrously difficult to tolerate. Them. Staring at *her*. Mesmerized by the soft colors of her and the shape of her face. I open the door and lift her, carrying her out of the truck, to get some distance. *She's mine.*

"Bo, you can put me down now," she says.

I don't. I kick the door of the truck shut and start carrying her up the stairs of my house as the boys drive back down the driveway.

"Bo?"

"I will. As soon as we get inside. We can't be too careful."

She's watching me as I carry her, like she's confused by my caveman schtick. Come to think of it, *I'm* confused by my caveman schtick. And by how fucking *voracious* it is. Like I've morphed into a goddamn sasquatch or something.

I really don't care.

I'll tone it down as much as I'm capable of, but there's only so much toning down I can *do*. All those years of waiting, all that pent-up energy, all that angst and doubt and wondering if I'd ever find someone even a fraction as perfect as *this*, has now converged into one blazing supernova of obsession.

I'll keep her safe.

When she'll let me, I'll take her to bed and make sweet, hot, endless love to her every day and every night for the rest of time. Or I'll die trying.

And eventually, starting now, I'm going to try to figure out how to get her to fall in love with me.

Chapter Seven

Millie

My heart's beating fast, pumping adrenaline through my veins. I'm being carried into the biggest house I've ever seen by the hottest *guy* I've ever seen, while crowds of people chant my name from behind a distant iron gate.

What the hell is going on? Did a random cosmic comet sprinkle stardust all over my life?

I'm staying here tonight.

With him.

I don't even know him.

He's incredibly *intense*, but in a way that makes me feel like he'd take a bullet for me. Which makes no sense. Men are usually *shooting* metaphorical bullets at me, not blockading me from stuff that could potentially harm me. It's a plot twist I wasn't expecting. As for the carrying me around thing, if it was anyone else, I'd probably be pummeling him with my fists and demanding to be set free. With Bo, it's like all the little strands of my DNA are leaning in, breathing in the scent of his man-sweat and his superstar pheromones.

Wow, he smells good ... in a sweaty, beefed-up alpha sort of a way.

I have never in my life thought of a person as "alpha." But I do now.

At least there's an enormous stone wall and an alarm system with space-age blinking lights between us and the people who have, for reasons I can't even begin to understand, taken a rabid interest in me. Or, more accurately, Bo's five second brain freeze in the middle of the season's opening football game.

Hopefully some other meme will have diverted the town's interest by tomorrow morning. I'll go back to my dorm and Bo can get on with his life. The whole thing will fade into a distant one-off memory of that random time I spent an evening with a hot quarterback in his swanky mansion.

We go inside. Bo kicks the door closed and sets me down in the middle of a huge foyer area with a chandelier and a grand staircase.

"This place is amazing." It really is. It looks like a castle, but it has a lot of wood and glass which makes it feel modern and cool and sophisticated, like some genius architect spent weeks deliberating over every detail. Even from the entrance, you can tell as you look deeper into the house that it's full of clean lines and awesome spaces.

"It's a little too big for one person, but it's home," he says.

"Doesn't your family live here?" This place is big enough to house an entire village. Or sports team.

"My parents are both dead," Bo says. "My oldest brother Gage lives in Chicago and my other brother Caleb is doing a tour of duty in Afghanistan. He's due back next month."

"I'm sorry." About his parents, I mean.

Bo still has my backpack slung over his shoulder. He's watching me again with those crazy eyes. He looks big and tall and *masculine* as all get out. Like he has a lot of testosterone or whatever pumping through him. I'm reminded again that it's just me and Bo, alone here tonight. "Come on," he says. "I'll show you around."

He leads me into a giant, state-of-the-art kitchen. It has a wall of windows that look out onto what could only be described as an *estate*. There are lawns and fields in the distance and I can see a lake, and a dock. And another, smaller house next to the lake.

"Who lives in the lake house?"

"At the moment, no one. Caleb will probably use it when he gets back. It'll be a good place for him to decompress. He's recovering from shrapnel wounds from a bomb explosion."

"Wow."

Bo pulls his football jersey over his head and starts taking off his padding.

Okay, holy hell. His chest and shoulders and abs are, like, *outstandingly* buff and beautiful. His football pants are slung low on his lean hips and he has that defined muscular V thing that's sort of fascinating ... and an arrow line of dark hair.

Yikes.

I try not to stare. I don't have a lot of experience with men. *Especially men like this one,* it has to be said. I've avoided men like the plague my whole life because I spent most of my life watching them prey on my mother. I tried to protect her as much as I could, but she was an easy (and willing) target. Before she became an addict, she'd been a real beauty. But by the end, once the drugs had ravaged her, every detail of her beauty, inside and out, was just completely, terribly gone.

When the men who preyed on my mother saw me, things always turned bad. I got good at hiding, running, and defending myself. I bought myself two stun guns which look like flashlights but have high-powered shock buttons that work surprisingly well, especially when they're not expecting it. So I managed to walk away from my past relatively unscathed. Because I was vigilant about keeping my distance.

Because of all that, I'm used to feeling like I'm in danger. Now, it's very noticeable to me that my fight-or-flight mindset is completely ... absent. Not that Bo *couldn't* overpower me easily if he wanted to. He's watching me like he's thinking about it. He's got a ravenous hungry-wolf thing going on that's making his eyes practically glow.

But I'm not scared of him. There's a wavelength. Bo McCabe is fierce and clearly strong as hell, but I get this feeling that he'd hurt anyone and anything, including himself, before he'd ever hurt me.

It's reassuring.

He grabs a faded yellow t-shirt that's hung over a chair and pulls it on. "I'll show you the rooms upstairs. I have to leave early in the morning for practice but you can stay here and work. It's quiet."

"Thanks. But it's probably best if I head back to my room in the morning."

"There's no reason for you to rush back. You can work on your book undisturbed."

I'll admit that's a ridiculously appealing offer. From the two hours I spent there, my dorm seemed loud and crowded, especially since classes haven't started yet and all the new students are going insane with their newfound freedom. And the library seems like less of an option after the whole *going viral* fiasco.

I follow him into another large room that's obviously his man cave on steroids. There's a pool table, pinball machines, a poker table, darts, air hockey and a foosball table. The bar area is nicer than most bars I've seen (a lot, since my mother was a regular at all the local places near our trailer park), with stools, hanging glass racks, glass-fronted fridges and even taps with different types of beer. Another section has two gargantuan comfortable-looking couches, reclining lounge chairs and an enormous flat-screen TV. There's a wall of sliding doors that lead out onto a patio. I can see a modern-looking glassed-in pool area and a fire pit.

"Wow."

"Yeah. I basically live in this room and so does my team."

"I can see why. It's like man heaven."

He leads me up a back staircase and into a wide hallway with lots of doors leading off of it. He starts opening them. The house is a perfect blend of classic and modern. You can tell it was designed and also decorated by someone who had the kind of style most people only dream about. It's basically a work of art. "Choose any room you want," Bo says. "They all have their own bathrooms. But before you decide, I'll show you the attic in case you want that one."

At the far end of the hallway is another door. It's painted a soft shade of teal. I follow him up a narrow set of wooden stairs to a room that's its own floor, like a turret. He flicks on a light switch. Four lamps, a soft spotlight and a string of fairy lights turn on around the room.

I gasp. *Wow*. It's the cutest, coolest, most enchanting space I've ever seen.

There's a round window at the far end that's framed with decorative stained glass vines. A queen-sized bed sits in a romantic little nook under another stained glass window. There are bookshelves, sewing machines and boxes full of rolls of fabric and half-finished garments. There's an open door to a bathroom that looks just as tastefully luxurious as the rest of the house. There are lamps on tables and lots of art on the wooden walls. The ceilings are vaulted, giving the space an open, airy feel. Under the round window is a desk that looks out over the view. I can see the full moon reflecting off the mirror-calm surface of the lake.

"This was my mother's studio," Bo says. "She was a designer. She was starting to get some interest from a few of the big fashion houses."

There's a framed photo of a young, gorgeous, dark-haired woman on one of the bookshelves. I walk over to take a closer look. "Is this her?"

"Yes." There's another photo, of the same young woman and a man that looks a lot like Bo. In the photo, the two of them are by a pool. It's summer. They're staring into each other's eyes, laughing. They look impossibly happy. "My parents. We lost them around five years ago."

"I'm sorry, Bo. I lost my mother, too." I'm surprised I even mention that. It usually stays in its locked-up little fortress at the back of my mind. "At least they knew real happiness." I stare at the photo.

There's something absolutely riveting about it. I don't think I've ever felt as happy as these people look. *They're so in love with each other.* You can just tell. They're lost in their own little world.

I feel a weird pang of what might be jealousy. In actual fact, I've never thought to feel jealous about love before. I've never really thought about love much at all. Partly because I was dealing with other things. And partly because the whole idea of love seems a little too far-fetched. I've never really seen it. But here it is. Right here in this photo.

"What about your father?" Bo asks.

"He was out of the picture before I was born." In fact, he left town the morning after I was conceived never to be heard from again. I'd die before admitting this to Bo, but my mother once told me she'd been with two men that night, and she wasn't actually sure which one it was. My mother was what you might call a free spirit, even before she got trapped inside a hell pit of opioid addiction.

Bo leans against the leather couch and sets my bag down. His strong-looking, tanned, hair-dusted arms flex as he folds them. His t-shirt pulls tight over the hard planes of his broad chest and his burly shoulders.

Holy smokes. He really is beautiful.

He catches me looking at him and I blush. "And your mother?" he says. "What happened?"

What to say? I hate talking about this.

He seems to sense something about my silence. "Mine died tragically, too. And my father took his own life soon after. It never gets any easier. I know. You don't have to explain anything."

How awful that must have been for him. "She died of a heroin overdose," I admit to him. "It wasn't her first."

His blue gaze holds mine. Some people can be judgmental about stuff like addiction. There's not a thing about heroin that's cool or fun or glamorous. It's all about desperation, death and total destruction. But Bo just says, "That must have been really fucking hard to deal with."

"It was. Like it would have been for you, too."

"How long had she been an addict?"

"Around eight years, off and on. Mostly on. She sprained her ankle, that's all it was, walking down the steps of our trailer." I feel the heat rise to my face. I don't usually tell people I grew up in a trailer park. I don't know why I'm telling him now. Here, in this to-die-for mansion, we could be in a different universe than the one I travelled from only days ago. But I'm this deep in to it now, so I keep going. "Just a swollen ankle that wasn't even broken. The doctor gave her some Oxy for the pain and that was it. She kept refilling her prescriptions until it became too expensive. So she found something cheaper. And much stronger."

"I'm sorry. It sucks. We had a few overdoses in our high school."

"Yeah. Mine, too. I tried to help her. We did everything we could think of. Rehab. Therapy. But it never made a difference. She never got better. Only worse." I hate dredging all this back up again. "Anyway, it's all in the past now. I don't know why I'm even talking about it."

"Because it helps sometimes."

A whole conversation passes between us, without words. It's strange. It's almost like he gets something about me that no one else ever has.

Even so, I'm glad when he doesn't ask any more questions about it.

He stands up and walks over to his mother's desk. He flicks on the lamp that's standing next to it, which casts a golden light. "She used to say she got her best ideas sitting right here. This room is yours if you want to use it for your writing. Any time you want. I'm sure she would have liked that."

It's kind of ... the absolutely perfect place to sit and write a novel. Or at least work on it for a few hours tomorrow, while he's at football practice. I guess the room could feel spooky, with all those memories hanging around, but it doesn't. Besides, I'm used to ghosts. This room feels more like it's infused with layer upon layer of raw, emotional inspiration. "Thank you, Bo. I'd love to."

I almost wish I could get started now, but my stomach makes a growling sound, which makes me blush again.

Bo smiles and stands up. "I can't have my guest going hungry, now, can I? I'll go take a quick shower then I'll make us something to eat. I'll meet you at the bar in twenty."

I smile back at him. Because I'm here in this perfect room in this perfect house in this perfect town. *With this perfect football hero.* It's hard to adjust to the overload. "Okay."

Bo leaves me to it and makes a stern face at me before disappearing down the staircase. "Don't be late."

"Yes, boss."

Once he's gone I wander around, looking at the art. And the many boxes of unfinished projects. *Don't waste your time,* this space is whispering. *Squeeze every drop out of the life you've been given. Make it good before it's too late.*

I go over to my bag and slide my laptop out. I set it on the desk and open it. I sit in the chair and bring up the document I'm working on.

And I start to write. It's like the floodgates have opened. My fingers can't keep up with my ideas, which pour onto the page in a feverish rush. For the next half hour, I completely lose myself.

I jump a little when I hear something.

"Hey."

I turn and Bo's leaning against the doorframe with his brawny shoulder resting against one side and his hands in his pockets. He's wearing an old pair of jeans and a clean white shirt, which emphasizes his tan. His hair is still damp from his shower and has been smoothed into place.

Holy hell. He's absolutely stunning.

He walks over to me. "Press 'Save'," he says.

"It saves automatically."

"Then press 'off.' When's the last time you ate something?"

I think about it for a second. "Breakfast. At a truck stop in Kentucky." I already have this habit of telling Bo things I wouldn't tell other people.

Once my computer's off, Bo scoops me up into his arms.

"Bo—"

"This is what I do when I'm rescuing you."

"What are you rescuing me from this time?"

"Starvation." He carries me over to the door and down the narrow staircase, taking care with me, so I don't get bumped. He smells clean and minty and outdoorsy. Like sunshine and green grass mixed with that heady cocktail of those alpha male pheromones, go figure.

As much as I appreciate him making dinner, his *aggressiveness* is a little overwhelming. "Has anyone ever told you you're kind of a control freak?"

"I'm a quarterback. Of course I'm a control freak."

He grins at me, like he's daring me to defy him. Just from the look on his face, I can't help almost forgiving him.

We get down to the bar and he sets me on a bar stool. There are two plates piled high with food. There's silverware, napkins and two full glasses of champagne along with a bottle on ice.

"I hope you like hamburgers and French fries. And champagne."

"I love hamburgers. And French fries. I've never had champagne."

"It's French. To go with the French fries." He clinks his glass against mine and takes a sip. "That's a joke, by the way."

"What are we celebrating?"

"We won the first game of the season. You're going to write a kick-ass book. And you're here."

That last line comes out sounding kind of deep and his eyes do that smoldering thing again. I take a sip of the champagne. It tastes good. And expensive.

The crazy thing is: I *like* being here. It's the nicest, calmest, most welcoming place I've ever been. It feels safe, and much more than that. It feels like the kind of place a person could not just survive, but thrive. For the first time in a long time, I don't feel scared. At all. I feel *alive*, like Bo's presence has turned me electric and hyper-aware. Music pulses through the surround sound system and the TV is playing a football game on mute.

The truth is, I feel more comfortable with this hunky quarterback than I have with anyone for a long time. Maybe *ever*. Which probably says a lot about the life I've led, who knows. It doesn't make sense, but it's true.

For a few seconds I just let myself take it all in. I'm not sure how my life took such a gargantuan U-turn over the past few days but I don't bother analyzing it. I've decided that tonight I'm just going to go with it.

He clinks his glass against mine again. "To waiting," he says.

Bo's blue eyes spangle. He's watching me. I know what he means. He's been saving himself, Violet said. Not that it matters, but so have I, most likely for very different reasons. Maybe it's the champagne, but I can't help it: I wonder if his thick hair is as soft as it looks. I wonder what it would feel like to kiss him. I've never once been kissed.

Which is a strange thing to think about with a total stranger who I've known for a total of ... an hour? Maybe two? Something about Bo McCabe—and it wouldn't take a rocket scientist to figure out what, considering his entire package is above and beyond anything I've encountered in my lifetime—is taking my thoughts in new directions.

"What's your last name?" he says.

"Baylin. Millie Baylin."

"Middle name?"

"I don't have one."

"No?" His eyebrows furrow, like he's upset that someone didn't do their job well enough. Which is true enough.

"What about you?"

"Jack."

"Bo Jack McCabe," I say. "Or are you, like, Beauregard or something?"

He laughs. I like the sound of his laughter. It's deep and has a crazy, infectious edge. "No. Just Bo."

He's watching my eyes and ... all right, I can admit he's ... *extremely* attractive. Not just on the outside, but everything else about him, too. With his bizarrely intense devotion to giving me everything I need, he's making me feel less out of place than I probably should. "Well, Millie Baylin. It's nice to meet you."

"Nice to meet you too, Bo McCabe." I think about what it'll be like to be acquaintances or even friends with Bo. To go to the occasional football game. To run into him every now and then around campus. Will it be enough? I already have this feeling it won't be enough, for either one of us. But I can't even go there. Not yet. To be honest, I don't know if I'll *ever* be ready to go there. Maybe my baggage is too heavy to cast aside to jump head first into something that promises to be way too good to be true. The brief, small glimpses of *too good to be true* I've seen in my life have always turned out to be exactly that.

I'll thank him for the meal, I'll stay the night, maybe spend a few hours enjoying the peace and quiet of his beautiful house tomorrow before I brave the dorm and whatever's left of my fifteen minutes of fame, which is hopefully now over. End of story.

Turns out, it was never going to be that simple.

Chapter Eight

Fucking hell.

I think I might be having some kind of freaky out-of-body experience. Everything about me is screaming *MINE*. I've regressed into full-on knuckle-dragging mode and I don't give a fuck.

I want her.

I want everything.

She's mind-numbingly pretty. She doesn't look real, she's so stunning. Like a woodland creature who's lost her way and is still shell-shocked by the sudden daylight. She's shy. Unsure. Which is understandable. Her life has been hell, you can tell by the spooked shadows behind her eyes.

All that's over now.

I'm going to make sure of it.

My lust is raw and obsessive but it's more than that. Being this close to her is energizing me. I feel hypnotized and fully addicted to the shape of her mouth, the curl of her eyelashes, the lightning-bolt shade of her eyes.

I've found her. She's here. And she's more perfect than anything my lame imagination could have dreamed up.

It doesn't make sense. Except that it makes perfect sense. For the first time in five years, everything makes perfect sense.

My challenge now is to *not* go completely ballistic and scare her away or fuck this up in any way whatsoever. Patience, steady nerves and the ability to plan and carry out successful tactics are attributes I have.

When I'm playing football.

Can I keep my cool enough to convince this girl she's mine?

My father once told me he fell in love with my mother the very first time he saw her. That, in that exact moment, he was ruined for anyone else. A lot of people laughed when he told them that, but not me. Some people are just hardwired that way. For *knowing*. For caring about something real and for having the guts to admit it and to grab it with both hands and give it everything you've got.

Which is exactly what I intend to do.

I top up our glasses. She's almost finished her glass of champagne and her pale cheeks have little flags of pink, which is fucking adorable. She's so *colorful*. Even in her drab clothes, her surreal pink-tinted hair and the bright spark in her eyes glimmer.

"We have another game on Monday night," I tell her. "I want you to come. I'll get you VIP seats."

"Bo, that's nice of you to offer. But I can't. I have the book deadline and everything."

"I'll get you a box. You can bring your roommate and anyone else you want. You can come with me and I'll make sure no one bothers you."

A hint of a smile doesn't quite surface. She shakes her head a little. "Why would you even want me there? I'm an introverted book worm who's spent half my life trying not to step on spent needles. You'd be better off with a happy-go-lucky cheerleader from your own neighborhood."

She clearly doesn't know me very well. But she'll learn. "I'm not interested in the cheerleaders."

"I'm glad we're friends, Bo. Really. But on Monday night I'll be holed up in my dorm room with the door locked and my headphones cranked up. I've told you all this."

I don't answer at first. I'm not sure how to tell her that things aren't really going to play out like she thinks they might. I'm not a stalker and I'm not a bully. But I've just been plugged in to a lightning bolt. She can't expect me not to burn.

She bites her lip and looks up at me. My heart hurts because she's just so incredibly pretty. There's a little scar above one of her eyebrows. And her sprinkling of freckles is uneven. There are more on her right cheek than her left. These little imperfections—if you could even call them such a thing—slay me even more.

I grab the bottle of champagne and put it under my arm. Then I carefully take her glass. I stand up and start walking toward the door.

"Where are you going?"

"Where are we going, you mean?" I nod toward the door. "Come on."

She makes a face, like she's exasperated with me. Which is exactly what I want. I want her to *feel*. Anything at all. She starts following me. It's probably a good thing she does. Because if she didn't, I'll pick her up and carry her again. Or sling her over my shoulder like a goddamn caveman and take her upstairs.

"Where are *we* going, then?"

I lead her through the glass corridor that leads to the pool area. The hot tub is raised, in its own corner, surrounded by glass and tropical plants and some cushioned loungers and a rack of towels. It has a nice outlook out over the lake. It's warm in here. Tropical. "We're going to finish this champagne while we sit in the hot tub. Because there's no reason not to."

"Bo," she says, as though I've lost my mind. Her eyelashes are long, dark at the roots and almost gold at the curled ends. Usually girls wear a shitload of makeup, and it always confuses me. Why so much? What are they trying to look like? With Millie, I really don't think she's wearing any makeup at all. And she looks like *this*. Like she stepped out of a daydream at dawn, all dewy and fresh and flushed and unreal. "I'm not sitting in the hot tub with you."

"Why not?"

"Because."

"'Because' isn't a reason."

"Because I hardly know you. Because I'm already a little bit drunk and I need to go to bed."

"You can sleep tomorrow. You'll have the whole place to yourself."

"I don't have a bathing suit."

I set the champagne and the glasses on the side of the hot tub. I turn on the jets. Then I strip down to my boxers and get into the hot tub. Her eyes get wide. And so they probably should. I turn my back to her but the beast probably hasn't escaped her notice. My ongoing problem has gone into goddamn super-powered overdrive. "Neither do I."

I lean back against a couple of the jets, which makes the bubbles fizz up around my shoulders. If she walks out, I'll go after her. I'll bring her back. *She's here. She's sweet as fuck. And she's mine.* Now I just need to convince her of that. "We're young and free and you just started college," I say. "Against the odds, by the sound of it. It's time for you to start having some fun."

She's glaring at me. She's mildly pissed off because I don't care about her protests and it's the cutest thing I've ever seen. The entire world will probably tell me I'm wrong or it's too quick and how can I know for sure, but it doesn't matter. My obsession has already become part of my heartbeat, fueling it, heating the blood in my veins—*and my painfully engorged cock*—to inferno-levels.

I might already be in love.

More insistently in this exact moment, I'm *in lust*. The kind of hundred-proof lust that won't be reasoned with. The kind that cares about real feeling but is more concerned with taking *everything* in its blazing wildfire of pleasure and pain.

"Time to start living your life and making the most of it." I tip back my glass, emptying it. "Seems like you've got some lost time to make up for."

And so do I.

"You're probably right," she says.

"Of course I'm right."

She rolls her eyes, but there's a hint of a smile. "Let me guess. You're always right."

I grin at her and shrug. "I'm the quarterback. I have to be right."

This makes her laugh despite her kittenish annoyance and, *fuck*, I'm a goner.

"Close your eyes," she says.

I do, sort of. I hear the rustle of her clothes as she drops them, then feel the movement of water as she climbs into the hot tub.

Fuck fuck fuck.

My cock is hard and hot, throbbing with her nearness, like it's got a mind of its own. It takes all the willpower I possess not to ease her onto my lap right now. But I have to take this slow, or she'll run from me.

I open my eyes, slowly losing my mind. My girl, the one I've been waiting for, who just stepped out of some crazy-ass techno-colored fantasy beyond anything I could have hoped for, is in my hot tub, wearing only a lacy little bra and her panties.

Keep your cool, man. Keep your fucking head.

I place her glass of champagne in her hand. "Drink it."

"Are you trying to get me drunk?"

She's got a quirky little sense of humor that's killing me. "I'm trying to make you happy," I say, meaning every word. "And I haven't even gotten started."

Millie eyes me, like something about what I've just said hits some buried emotion. But then she smiles shyly and takes another sip.

Ten inches of pure, raging agony is having its way with me. Now that I've finally found her, all those years of going without are literally testing the boundaries of my sanity. I try to relax against the jets of the hot tub. She's watching me. Her silver gaze wanders across my face and my chest. She can check me out as much as she wants. She can take as much time as she needs.

Within reason.

In fact, the more she watches me, the crazier I feel.

She twirls a strand of her hair around her finger. I simply can't stop myself. Carefully, I replace her finger with mine. Her hair is even softer than it looks.

"Is this real?"

I'm referring to the color of her hair, of course, but I may as well be asking about the all of it. The face. The lips. The electric eyes. The absurdly flawless skin. The swell of her wet breasts at the surface of the water—*oh, fucking hell, she's dizzyingly plush and sweet and mouth-watering.*

"Yeah. My mother had red hair. My father ... well, it's anyone's guess."

I gently tug on the strand of her hair, pulling her closer.

"Bo ..."

"Millie ..."

"I'm not ..." Her breasts rise and fall gently with her breath.

"It's okay. I'm sure enough for both of us."

Her eyebrows quirk, but she lets me slowly ease her closer.

And closer.

137

When she's close enough, I hold her there for a few seconds, savoring the final moments of anticipation. But I've waited long enough.

I kiss her soft, soft lips.

Chapter Nine

Millie

Bo's mouth eases over mine. He makes a low, savage sound that, for some reason, excites some secret desire in me I never knew about until now. It's crazy-strong and unruly. I almost try to pull back but his hands are holding me in place. He won't let me disengage.

Bo's lips are gentle, but at the same time not gentle at all. Sure. Hungry beyond belief. And when his tongue touches mine, a wild, uncontrollable craving takes hold.

Wow.

Kissing is so intimate. He tastes *so good*. Like that scent of him. Delicious and irresistible. His hot, alpha appeal is flooding into me.

So this is what lust feels like.

Our tongues tangle and slide.

Maybe it's the champagne that's loosening some boundary in me, or maybe it's Bo himself. My mouth is hungry to taste him. My body feels soft and slippery. Bo sucks gently on my tongue, and a wave of heat ripples through me. I feel reckless. I want to taste more of him. My hands weave into the wet strands of his hair.

His hair is thick silk. His lips are champagne. His body is big and wet and unbelievably hard.

He's murmuring my name, dipping his tongue into my mouth like I'm the sweetest fruit he's ever tasted. *God.* Bo's fingers slowly brush along the skin of my stomach. I don't stop him. Some sort of wave is building. I'm already riding it. His hands are on my hips, gripping me. He's being gentle but there's a brimming power to him that's unmistakable. The realization of how strong he is, instead of scaring me, has the opposite effect. The grip of his fingers feeds a current of lust straight to the low pit of my stomach. And lower. A warm pulse takes hold inside me. Each sweet, molten throb makes me feel wilder. There's an edge of desperation. Because it's not enough, not nearly enough.

The feel and taste of him feed a pure, feral fire that pulls me in and won't let go. I've crossed over some threshold. I don't want to be afraid, or hide, or be alone.

I want to get closer to him. I want to *feel* him because nothing has ever felt this good.

Bo lifts me out of the water and carries me, dripping, over to the cushioned loungers, which are pushed together. Like a bed. His mouth never disengages. His tongue never pulls out of my mouth.

He lays me down and slides his big body up against mine. *Over mine.*

I should stop this. We're getting carried away.

If I could, I would. But my cravings won't let me. My pulse, *there,* doesn't *want* him to pull away. It wants him closer. *Much closer.* It wants more of his tongue and the sweet, warm hunger he's filling me with. My fingers ease through his thick hair, exploring the outstanding, rough, masculine textures of him. His scratchy square jaw. His corded neck. His hard, muscular shoulders.

Bo's hands slide up my body. He plays with the clasp of my bra. He unhooks it and it falls away. Instead of protesting, I wrap my arms around his neck as he kisses me. My nipples brush against the hair-dusted surface of his chest and I gasp. He holds my face in his hands and kisses me, his lust fueling mine to fever-pitch.

Our kisses get bolder, deeper.

You're so beautiful. I can't believe how beautiful you are. I've waited so long for you.

He's as delirious as I am. We're too far gone to stop. Our slippery bodies slide against each other. Our ravenous need has sunk its teeth into both of us. My whole body is melting. I'm warm and wet. I suck on Bo's tongue and he groans. He licks his tongue into my mouth like he's starved for me. His fingers find my breasts and he rolls my nipples tenderly, until I moan.

Bo starts kissing a line down my neck, tasting me, sucking my nipple into his mouth.

Oh my God.

The sensation is overwhelming. He feeds on me in lusty, rhythmic pulls. It's the most intimate thing that's ever happened to me. Each tug of his mouth sends a dart of sensation straight to my *pussy*, which feels soft and tingly. I've never felt anything like this. Not even close. Like I might die if he stops or pulls away. All I can comprehend through my lust-drowsed haze is how good he feels.

He's kissing a line down my stomach, licking and kissing my skin.

Millie. Fuck, you're gorgeous. You taste so fucking good.

His fingers ease over my wet panties.

I squirm. I'm not protesting, but it's *so much.* His mouth is on me, kissing me *there*, through the wet, thin cotton of my panties and it feels so good I just let him. I can't resist the pleasure he's giving me. He moves my panties to the side. There's a pull against my hip and then they're gone. *Oh God, he ripped them off.* His tongue licks the soft lips of my pussy. *Oh.* Something's happening. A swelling warmth that's going to kill me with pleasure. He dips his tongue between the delicate folds of my pussy and finds the hyper-sensitive nub. He plays it with his tongue, sucking it in to the warm fire of his mouth.

Bo. Oh, God, Bo, I hear myself moaning.

Fuck, you're sweet, he's murmuring. He sucks on my clit and his fingers touch me, skating and rubbing, until the pleasure is simply too much. It's unendurable. The pleasure shatters into a wave of silky spasms that clench gently around his tongue as he licks into me.

He licks me until the ripples begin to calm. Then Bo climbs up next to me. He smooths my hair back from my face and stares into my eyes as he—*oh my God*—pushes something hard and *huge* against my still-rippling pussy. *It's happening again.* The pleasure wave is rushing back, even bigger this time.

I know what it is. I'm not completely naïve. I'm pinned under his weight and I can't see it but I know *his enormous cock is pushing against me*. It's hard but silky and wet and it feels so good the wave is just about to flood me again with its devastating pleasure.

I want it to.

At the edges of my delirium I know we're moving much too fast. I don't care. I don't try to stop him. I can sense that he might not be *able* to stop, even if I asked him to. In the lust-daze of my mind, this *thrills* me beyond belief. I want to let him do whatever he wants. Our bodies are so wet, so eager. The broad end of his cock is gliding silkily over my clit and the slippery rub pushes me over the edge. The pleasure is mind-blowing. My pussy starts to clench as Bo's massive cock starts pushing into me. At first it's sort of stuck there. I'm too tight. But he uses our wetness and the clench of my pleasure to slide his thick bulk deeper. And deeper. There's pain at the edges of the stunningly intense wave of bliss.

He slides himself out a little, then in, and in, stretching me open as I come around him.

"Millie. You feel so fucking perfect."

He kisses me and I can taste *myself* on his lips. It's astoundingly intimate, like he's claimed me already. Bo thrusts again. He's growling, lifting me, gripping me, invading me with slow, measured aggression. His big cock rubs against a sweet, aching trigger and the melting wave overflows *again*. My pussy clenches lusciously around him, milking every inch of his thick length until his cock starts jerking violently inside me. The pulsing thickness of his cock and the hot jets of his cum trigger more of those spiraling waves of pleasure. *I never knew a person could come this much. I thought it was supposed to hurt the first time.* Instead, I'm grinding and squirming to feel every inch of his spilling beauty.

Our climax is so intense it takes a while for us to come down from it. He's on top of me. My arms and legs are wrapped around him. We're breathing hard and our hearts beat in rhythm. He kisses my lips as I gaze up at him. His hands are weaved into my hair. His slick, slow-pulsing cock is deep inside me.

"Millie," he murmurs, kissing me again. "*I found you. My girl. Mine.*"

We lay like that for a long time, entranced, staring into each other's eyes. We're in a daze, lulled by the lingering effects of our rush, entwined like we can't bear to be separated. I never expected this. To feel like not just my body has connected deeply with his, but also my soul.

It sounds strange, but I've never felt so complete as I do now, with Bo deep inside me. His cock is hard again, filling me entirely, like he's taken full possession of me.

He holds his weight so he's not crushing me. I love how big he is, and how strong. He touches his fingers to my cheek, like he's making sure I'm real. He kisses my lips.

I want to stay right here inside you forever, baby, he whispers. *My Millie.*

I gasp as he thrusts his hard bulk deeper. This time we go slow. My arms and legs are still wrapped around him. His cock is so big and so thick, thrusting in a lazy but demanding rhythm as his tongue dips into my mouth. I start to come again. My pussy clamps snugly around him as I suck on his tongue. The wet, tight constriction of my body working his big cock makes him come again too, and he groans like his heart's breaking. I can feel the throbbing pulses as his cum gushes deep inside me.

I'm dazed with pleasure and sweet, sated lust. I want to hold him and taste him and keep him inside me. So I do. I play with his hair and kiss his lips and whisper in his ear to tell him how good he feels.

Much later, still half-dazed with pleasure, I vaguely notice the purple line at the horizon. It's reflecting off the still water of the lake. He's wrapped a blanket around us and I'm curled on my side, comforted by warmth and sleep, entirely enveloped in Bo's protective embrace. Bo's spooning me. His hot, heavy cock is wedged deep inside me. He's kissing my neck, licking me in lusty, gentle nips. His arms are wrapped around me. His hand fondles my breast. He teases my soft nipple between two fingers, rolling gently until it hardens into a tight little bud. Then he moves to the other breast, doing the same, touching them with the span of his fingers, playing. As he does this, his cock slides deeper. His fingers skate across the slippery lips of my pussy, fingering my clit, caressing me with languid tenderness. The pleasure, again, is crazy. I just never expected there to be so *much* of it. I arch back against him, squeezing, teasing. I want to make him come again.

He growls when I retreat the tiniest bit and grips me harder, driving as deep as he can go. *You're mine now, baby. I'm never letting you go.*

His words, delivered as they are along with the thick, impaling pleasure of his cock forcing its way inside, shatter me. The pulsing glow blooms, and my inner muscles clench strongly around him until the jetting warmth of his cum floods me and spills, wetting my thighs.

Nothing will ever feel as good as this. Nothing could ever feel as good as he does.

I open my eyes.

"Hey." He's sitting next to me, dressed in football gear.

"Hi."

Wow, I slept so deeply. I sit up a little, but the blanket falls to my waist and I realize I'm not wearing any clothes, so I lay back down.

Holy shit. It's all coming back to me.

Bo McCabe.

I lost my virginity to the ultra-sexy quarterback last night, only a few hours after meeting him and getting mobbed by his fans, then had hot, unprotected sex with him all night long. Very amazing, mind-numbingly orgasmic *hot sex.*

Wow.

I'm sore. I can feel muscles in places I didn't even know there *were* muscles.

No wonder.

He smiles at me, his alpha arrogance softened at the edges by ... happiness. He's *happy.* And hotter than ever. His hair is a glorious mess and, against the rugged handsomeness and the big, built masculinity, is sort of

... to die for. I have the urge to grab handfuls of it. *He's so damn beautiful.*

"You okay?" In the morning light, his blue eyes glimmer.

"Yes," I admit. "You?"

He grins. "I can definitely say I have never been better."

I can't help smiling sort of guiltily at him.

Bo laughs and lifts me onto his lap, bundled in my blanket. He's so freaking *strong*. And he's playful this morning. His intensity has a lightness to it that might have something to do with a long list of multiple orgasms. I lost count somewhere around six.

He touches his thumb to my bottom lip. It's a possessive gesture. Then he tilts his head to claim my mouth, like he can't resist. After an astoundingly tender kiss, he pulls back. "We need to talk about my— our—extreme case of throwing all caution to the wind."

Yeah, we did kind of do that. "I'm on the pill, by the way."

He blinks at me and his expression is sincere, with a caring edge. And something else. Something darker that's harder to read. "You are?"

"Yes."

"I guess that's a good thing. But why?"

Bo knows a few things about me but not all that much. He knows I am—*was*—a virgin. Somewhere in the middle of our frenzy last night, I remember him wiping my virgin blood from me along with his cum before he kissed me and pushed himself inside me again.

I don't answer right away. But I decide to be honest with him. That's just the way it seems to be between us. "I was underweight. It helped keep my cycle on track."

There's something behind his expression. Maybe pain at what I just told him. He holds my face. "I'm going to take such good care of you," he whispers.

I don't cry, but I almost could. For a lot of reasons.

Bo kisses me and the kiss turns hot and erotic. "I am so late, but I don't care. The girl of my dreams is naked and sweet and wet and so fucking luscious I can't leave without saying good morning properly." He lays me back and starts feasting on me. Like last night, any flickering thoughts about protesting are swept away by a tidal wave of lust as he sucks on my nipples, moving lower in a slow frenzy of crazy hunger. Also like last night, he seems to be able to give me orgasms at the drop of a hat. He makes me come hard with his mouth and his fingers. He's unlacing his pants and—*oh, Jesus*—it's the first time I've seen *all of him* in broad daylight. No wonder I'm so sore. The thing is *colossal*. Hot-looking and leaking with his pre-cum.

"Wrap your legs around me," he says.

Oh God. I do it. He touches the head of his giant erection against me. I know this will hurt but, somehow, just that hard, slippery touch tips me into yet another nearly unendurable orgasm.

How does he do that? The thing is a magic sex wand.

As he feels my pussy starting to pulse around the head of his cock, he slides his thick length all the way to the hilt and I cry out. But the pain only makes the pleasure more intense, if that's possible.

He moves with me, and as he does, still in his football gear, his hand loosely around my neck as he stares deep into my eyes, I feel him tremble with the intensity of this sudden, uncontrollable passion. Our wet, skewering bond has an emotional undercurrent.

His head drops and I can feel the coarse silk of his hair against my cheek. "*Oh, fuck, Millie, you feel too good.*"

He's trying to be careful with me, but he's too far gone. He thrusts harder, then he holds himself deep inside me and shudders, his big body jerking, and the flooding throb of his cock sets me off again. I moan his name. My muscles contract tightly around his beating length as he rocks into me.

We're breathing hard. His face is buried in my neck.

We lay like that for a while as our bodies flutter wetly in a secret rhythm. His mouth and the grip of his fingers will probably leave marks. *I'm glad. I want him to leave his marks on me.*

"Holy hell," he murmurs.

Yeah. Holy hell is right.

Bo lifts his head. He kisses me slowly and the kiss feels significant.

Too significant. What's happening to us? This is way too quick.

"Are you going to get in trouble for being late?"

He smiles and pulls himself out of me. I can feel his cum spill from my body. It's a strange feeling. *I love that he's been inside me. I don't want him to leave.* "Yes. But some things are more important."

He uses a towel to clean us. Then he tucks himself back into his pants and ties them. He wraps the blanket more securely around me.

"I don't want to go, but I need to at least show up."

"Of course, Bo. I'll be fine."

"You can swim and write. There's plenty of food in the fridge. I'll be back in a few hours."

"Okay."

"Millie?"

"Yeah?"

"I know this is all happening at warp speed. But don't be scared of it. Of me. Last night, and now … " He seems almost lost for words. "You're beautiful. So beautiful."

"You are too, Bo."

He touches two fingers to my lips, then to his heart. It might be the most heartfelt gesture I've ever seen, and it *hurts* for some reason. It *is* too quick. We've jumped in at the deep end, when I don't even know how to swim. I don't regret anything, but we can't really believe there's more to this than an explosive chemistry and one hell of an all-nighter, can we? I can't calibrate anything more than that, now that it's daylight and he's leaving and everything's taking on the tint of normality. Last night feels like a beautiful dream.

Bo stands up, walking backwards until he gets to the door. He gives me a bereft look, like he's torn. "I'll see you soon."

And then he's gone.

After Bo leaves, I stare out at the view for a while. It's such a beautiful place. The fields and the serene lake. There's a little house on top of the dock, with chairs in it. A small boat is moored and tied on a sandy beach. The lake house looks bigger than it did in the dark. It has two wings off the main part of the house and a large deck overlooking the lake.

It feels strange to be here alone.

I decide to swim in the pool, to wash off. I'm sticky. *With Bo's cum, and mine, and streaks of my virgin blood.*

Wow.

It's disorienting, as the magnitude of what happened sinks in. I don't regret it, not at all. It's just a lot to think about, as my mind retraces ... everything.

The pool is heated and the water's warm.

I get out and dry off with a plush towel. *The luxury of this place.* I don't think I could ever get used to it.

Then, because my clothes are bunched up on the floor, wet, I grab Bo's white shirt that's draped over the towel rack by the hot tub. It hangs down to the middle of my thighs, like a mini-dress.

It smells like him. I hold the collar to my face and inhale a long breath.

God.

That scent. His sunshine-and-alpha natural cologne could be bottled as an aphrodisiac and make him a fortune.

I hang my clothes over a heated railing to dry, then I go into the kitchen. Bo made coffee and it's still warm so I pour myself a cup. Then I eat some fruit and a piece of toast.

I make my way through the bar and up the staircase to his mother's studio. My bag and my laptop are where I left them, and I go over to sit at the desk.

The room looks even more enchanting in daylight. The sun shines through the stained glass windows and colors everything with shards of red and green and gold.

I don't know what compels me to do it but I open up my first book, instead of my second. It's the one that's about to be published, the story of my mother's downward spiral and how it felt to watch it happen. *The wasting away of her health and her spirit. The men who used her. The spoons and the needles. The desperation and her sunken eyes. The bruises along her arms and then her ankles, and finally her neck, when the veins got too hard to find.* The story sucks me in. It's raw and emotional and it takes me straight back to a different time and place.

The place I left behind, in fact ... only three days ago.

I got here yesterday.

Yesterday. All that happened in *one day.*

The arrival, the dorm, the football game, the Jumbotron social media explosion.

Bo.

Something about the realization puts a lot of things into suddenly-clear perspective.

Why am I in his house? Alone? Wearing his shirt? Sitting at his mother's desk?

I shouldn't be here.

It was a magical night, there's no doubt about that. One that changed me. My first time might very well be the best time I'll ever have. It would be very hard to top that.

But it's just not realistic that there's anything more to it than lust. I don't care about his saving-himself intensity or whatever that was. So he saved himself. And now he's free to do whatever comes next. You don't fall in love at first sight on a Jumbotron. Real life just isn't like that.

I need to get back to my room, to get ready for classes to start and focus on what I came here to do.

Not get carried away by some hot-quarterback-and-his-fancy-mansion fantasy.

I don't like the thoughts that swirl through my head, but it happens sometimes.

You're trailer trash. What are you doing with a superstar? You don't belong here. He's a million miles out of your league and he always will be.

Best to recognize this for what it was: beautiful.

And over.

I close my laptop.

I slide it into my bag and pick up my hat, tucking my hair into it like I usually do. I take my phone from the pocket of my bag and book an Uber.

Then I go back down to the pool and change into my clothes, which are almost dry. I put my coat back on.

And I make my way out the door, down the long driveway. I find the button that releases a small gate that opens next to the main one. For walking through, instead of driving.

The Uber pulls up just as I get to the curb.

It was fun, Bo.

But it's best this way.

Chapter Ten

I'm driving way over the speed limit and my car screeches to a burning stop as I skid into my parking space. I'm an hour late. For good reason.

I've never missed a practice. Coach threatens all the time to bench me to make way for the sophomore punk who's up-and-coming. He goes on about how the kid needs more time on the field to get seasoned. It's a game Coach plays, to rile me, to keep me on my toes.

Draft picks are seven months away. I can't afford to get benched.

He launches straight into it. "Good of you to grace us with your presence, McCabe. Is this your idea of a goddamn joke?"

I glare at him levelly but it's not in my best interest to piss off my coach. "Sorry, Coach. Got tied up."

"By the Jumbotron Angel, pray tell?" Kirby elbows me.

"Fuck off."

"Your hair's a mess, Bo," smirks Tyler, before I can get my helmet on.

"Hallelujah!" hollers Kowalski, giving Tyler a high five. "He finally got laid."

"All of you can fuck off," I tell them, but it's no use. They howl and pat me on the back and make the most of it. I can't even bring myself to get pissed off.

My life is too *beautiful. She's* too beautiful. I still can't believe she's *real.* And in my house. And, *fuck,* just ... insanely perfect.

All the angst and pent-up aggression that have hounded me for years have taken a turn. To obsession. *I've found her. She feels like heaven. She tastes like nothing else on this earth.* All I want to do is get back to her, before I lose my mind. "Let's get this over with. There's someplace I need to be."

My team laughs some more but we get into position for a play we've been practicing.

For the next two hours, I play out of my skin. Turns out the little angel has another effect on me. I'm on fire. I've been touched by magic. I can't wait to touch a whole lot more of it.

"Play like that for the rest of the season," Coach says, "and you can name your price, Bo."

He never calls me Bo. He must be impressed.

We take a five-minute water break and I'm sitting on the bench. Kirby takes his phone out of his bag and checks it. "Hey, Bo. Look at this. Isn't this your angel?"

"What?" I stand up and grab his phone.

There's a photo of her. It's a video. She's on the green, walking toward her dorm, with her hat and coat on. *Right now*. People are swarming around her. A crowd is forming.

They're saying things to her.

She's trying to walk past them with her hat down low but *some guy grabs it* and pulls it off. Her hair spills out, shimmering in the sunlight.

She turns. She asks for it back. She's upset.

She's crying.

I don't even look back. I start running.

"Bo!" someone calls but I barely hear it. I get clear of the stadium and get into my car, peeling out, weaving my way through traffic toward the main part of campus. When I reach the edge of the green I pull up on the grass and jump out of the car. There's a huge crowd on the green now. More cars are pulling up behind mine. I vaguely realize it's my team. Some of them have followed me.

I push my way through the crowd.

"Hey," someone says angrily, then they look up. "*Oh.*"

"Oh my God, it's Bo."

The crowd starts parting for me.

I get to the middle, where three guys are blocking Millie's way. One of them is holding her hat.

"We googled you," one of them is saying. "You're from a trailer park in Florida."

"Your mother went to jail," another one says. "Her mugshot is online. Says she got arrested for breaking and entering and for possession of heroin. Is that true?"

"She was a junkie?" says the guy holding her hat. "Fuck."

"Are you and Bo a *thing*?" says the third one. "Does he know all this?"

"You're not just after Bo for his money, by any chance, are you?"

"Please," Millie's begging them. "Just give me my hat and let me—"

I don't hear the rest of it. Because I'm tackling the guy in the middle. The one who touched her. Who took something from her. He falls hard.

I see Kirby tackling one of the other guys. And Tyler manhandling the third one.

The guy under me is groaning.

I climb off him. I walk over and pick up Millie's hat off the ground, brushing some leaves off of it. I walk over to where she's standing. She looks so small.

Carefully, I place her hat on her head. I wipe her tears with my thumbs. Then I scoop her carefully into my arms.

Chapter Eleven

Bo takes me home. He carries me straight up to his room. He takes off my coat and most of his gear and he puts me into his bed. He leaves my hat on. He wraps his big body around me and he holds me as I cry.

I cry it all out. All of it.

I never cried when it was happening. Crying made me feel weak, like I couldn't handle what I needed to handle. But now it wants out. It wracks through me in wrenching sobs. My tears wet his chest and he just holds me and smooths my hair, crooning words to me. *You're okay now. I'm here with you and I'm going to take care of you. I'll give you everything you need to make you happy. You'll see. There's nothing stopping us now. Everything's okay.*

I cry until the tears dry up and there's nothing left.

Until the words he's murmuring almost sound like they could be true.

I climb up onto him. I gaze into his eyes. How is such a thing possible, to meet someone, to feel a connection that runs this deep, so, so quickly? You hear it described, how some people just "click." That's what's happened to us. Me and Bo *click*. Something about our souls is a match. Our broken pieces fit together. "You rescued me again," I tell him.

"I'll keep rescuing you as many times as you need to be rescued."

No one in my life has said the kind of things Bo says to me. "Why do you do it?"

"Because you rescued me first. I was starting to doubt everything about my life. And then I looked up and there you were."

I'm crying again, but for a different reason. "I don't know where you came from, Bo McCabe. But I think I like you."

He laughs softly. "I like you, too, Millie Baylin. A lot. Let's start with that and see where it takes us."

"I guess we could do that."

"We're *doing* that. We're doing it." He holds my face and kisses my lips softly. "I'm not happy with you, by the way, for walking out on me."

"I wanted to give you one last chance to be free of me. All those things those guys were saying were true." My mother's arrests always involved drama, mugshots and, apparently, a lingering online footprint. Sometimes I hate the internet.

"I don't care about that. It doesn't matter."

"None of it's glamorous. Addiction. Incarceration. Breaking and entering. Fraud."

"Neither is the stuff that happened to my parents. Your mother was sick. So was mine. Life can be messy. And hard. And cruel. But it can also be beautiful."

He's right. His sapphire eyes glimmer in the dim lighting of his room.

"*You're* beautiful," he says. "What's going on, right here, right now—*this* is beautiful. We're going to see where this leads us, because it feels good. It doesn't matter if it's happening fast. I *like* fast. I've waited a long time and all of it was slow. I'm *ready* for fast."

"But you can't know all this already, Bo, from a glimpse at a Jumbotron and … an amazing one night stan—"

"I *do* know it. I know it."

"How? How can you be so sure?"

"I don't know how I'm sure! I just am."

"But what if you're wrong? What if you get to know me and it turns out you don't even like me?"

He gives me an exasperated look. "That's not going to happen."

"You can't know that."

"Millie," he says slowly, as though I'm testing his infinite patience. "Everyone has to deal with getting to know each other. We've just jumped in at the deep end, that's all. We'll teach each other to swim as we're catching the perfect wave."

He really does have a way with words. "I've never even dated before. I don't know how."

"Neither have I. We'll learn."

"But—"

"We're friends, you said. Friends don't walk out on each other. Okay? Let's start with that."

Friends also don't romp nakedly by the hot tub and make love all night and give each other multiple simultaneous orgasms that are so mind-blowingly good and connective and real, it changes your outlook on everything, I want to point out. But he already knows that. I can see it right there in his ocean-blue eyes that he knows that.

"What your mother did isn't what *you* did, anyway. Look what you've already accomplished, even though it's probably been a lot harder for you than for most people. You've written a book that's about to be published. That's huge. You got into college and you're making things happen for yourself. You don't *need* to be rescued. You've rescued yourself. And you don't need anyone's approval. Not those idiots on the green. Not Instagram's. Not anyone's. You're wildly impressive."

Somehow, the things he's saying are leeching right into the fabric of my soul, like rainwater on parched earth.

"And you should let me indulge my obsession because if you don't, I'll follow you wherever you go."

"You will?" I whisper.

"Yes. I will."

All I really want to do is to trust him and give him everything he wants. If only it was that easy.

Maybe it is that easy.

Sometimes in life—although I've never done this until I met Bo McCabe—maybe you just have to go with it. Maybe you can't let fear hold you back and you have to be willing to get hurt to get to the good stuff. The real stuff. I decide he's worth the risk. "Okay."

His eyebrows lift. "Okay?"

"Okay," I confirm.

Bo kisses my face. My cheeks. My lips. "Okay." The way he says it sort of rings with hope. He's looking at me like he did that very first time, in the library. With such *sureness* it hurts my heart. *You*, that look is saying. His voice is low and husky. "I know you're wondering how I can be so sure when we don't know each other very well."

"I am."

"It's because everything I *do* know about you is nirvana to me. Your hair. Your smile. Your eyes. Your face. The way you make me feel when we're together. Everything. The more I learn, the more you slay me. I've been looking and hoping for you for such a long time, Millie, and now ... *here you are*. I don't want to waste time. I want to start right now."

My Bo is such a romantic.

"And I want you to promise me that you won't walk away from me again, without giving me a chance to change your mind."

"Shh," I whisper. "I'm not going to leave you. I'm here." Walking away just doesn't make sense. I want to try, too. I want to try with all my heart.

He kisses me, and that's all it takes, like always. His tongue glides over mine and the taste of him floods me with simmering lust. Bo's hands slide under my top, raising it over my head and tossing it aside. My hat falls off and my hair makes a curtain around our faces. We help each other pull off the rest of our clothes as his kiss finds deeper and more intimate angles. Until I'm naked, lying on top of his big, hard body.

The emotional commitment is complicated. *This* is the easy part. Our physical connection doesn't feel complicated at all. Maybe because we've both waited. We're *hungry*. The chemistry between us feels fiery and supercharged.

I kiss his chest. I love the rough, hair-dusted textures of him. Slowly, I kiss a line down the quilted muscles of his stomach, to the fascinating V.

He groans.

I *love* the V. I lick it. Then I touch my tongue to the arrow line of dark hair. I take his giant, rigid erection in my hands and I kiss the head, touching my tongue to the slit, drinking the drops of milky moisture. I suck on the round head of his cock until he's grasping the sheet with his fists.

There's a power to this that's sort of beguiling. My superstar alpha is completely at my mercy. I lick and suck gently on his cock, squeezing lightly with my hands, taking more of him in my mouth, until he groans my name. His cock jerks and he comes in hot, seedy bursts. I drink some but there's *a lot*. I lick him as his breathing begins to slow. I like the taste. It's *him*. His alpha elixir.

He pulls me up so I'm lying on top of him. "Am I dreaming?" he whispers, blinking at me.

"No," I gasp. Because he's sliding his still-semi-hard cock against my pussy. His cock is slippery with his cum. He pushes inside me, and his thickness slides deeper. He just came, but I know from last night that it won't take long for him to revive. Already, he's getting harder, filling me as he grips my hips. I'm sore, but the wetness of his cum and having him *already inside* as he hardens makes it bearable. Not just bearable. *Beautiful.* Everything about Bo McCabe is beautiful. I squeeze my muscles around him..

"Oh, fuck, Millie. I love the way you feel."

We rock into each other, holding each other like we can't get close enough. I can feel that he's fully hard again. His cock feels so incredibly big and deep inside me.

I want him there. I love him there.

The rocking motion of our connection rubs against a sweet spot deep inside me and I moan. He thrusts harder, even deeper, and I lose myself completely, shattering into silky spasms that work him and pull the pleasure from his cock in warm, gushing bursts.

It's disorienting, the *extremeness* of this pleasure. The deep connection Bo and I already seem to have feels bigger than merely physical. It feels emotional. Almost spiritual.

I don't like to think about what will happen to my heart if it doesn't work out between us—which, given the speed of our fall seems just as likely as us living happily ever after. If we're going to do this, which we're clearly already doing, it's a giant leap of faith, for both of us.

He seems to read my thoughts. "Don't break my heart, baby. You're holding it in your hands."

I'm sort of crying and laughing at the same time. His words lock everything in place. We *shouldn't* be on equal ground. He's a football hero who lives in a mansion. I'm ... not. With Bo, none of the stuff outside our little cocoon of lust and hope and fascination matters. In here, it's just our two broken souls fitting together in a way that makes me feel stronger than I ever have, not just because of him, but because of me. "I won't, Bo."

God, I hope I survive him.

Somehow I get the feeling we *will* survive. More than survive, but *thrive* in a way we never could without each other.

Somehow I get the feeling that he's the one.

Later, Violet comes over. She gives me a hug and I lead her into the bar area. "Violet, this is Bo. Bo, my new roommate Violet."

"Actually, I think she might be *my* new roommate." Bo smiles at her.

She places her hands on her hips. "How dare you steal my roommate! I like her." But then she laughs and gives him a sort of awkward hug.

"I like her, too." Bo grins at me. Then he says to Violet, "Spend as much time here as you want, Violet. Move in, if you want."

She finds this hilarious. "I'm not *moving in*."

Just then, six football players arrive. They pour into Bo's game room, making themselves totally at home. They're loud and huge and they help themselves to the beer on tap and the pool table and the TV. The music is turned up. They brought more food than I've ever seen. I recognize Shawn, Tyler and a few that I remember from the ride home last night, who Bo introduces as Kowalski and Gates, and there are two others, Bronson and Hayes.

"You're up, Violet," says Kowalski, holding out a pool cue. Violet's one of those people who can't help making any situation fun. She's bubbly and cute and more than one of these football players is watching her.

But she and Shawn are scrolling on his phone. "Shit, Bo," says Shawn, "you're going to need to post something on your Instagram. There's a mob of people outside your gate right now. The incident on the green this afternoon is flooding the internet."

"How'd you get away from Coach, by the way?" asks Bo.

Shawn shrugs. "He said if the Jumbotron Angel can inspire you to play like you did today, then she needs our undivided attention. He's insisting you get one of the VIP boxes, Millie, and that you attend every game."

"Yes!" squeals Violet. "Her new bestie will make sure of it. And keep her company, of course."

"See?" says Bo, pulling me against his big, buff body. "I need you with me."

He lifts me so I'm sitting on the bar. He stands between my knees and holds my face carefully in his warm hands. He doesn't care that they're all watching us. He's dressed in jeans and a blue shirt that hugs the sculpted muscles of his shoulders, and he's staring into my eyes like he can't tear his gaze away. Of course I'm captivated by his rugged perfection, as usual. But I notice, too, that his eyes are bloodshot. From the late night, maybe. And from the overload of emotion. More than anything else, as he leans in, he looks *happy*. He smiles at me and it's so sweet and heartfelt I feel it all the way down to those damaged pieces of my heart, which don't feel quite so damaged anymore.

I'm in love with him.

When he leans in to kiss me, even with all these people watching, I let him. I kiss him back.

It's strange how sometimes things don't work out.

And how sometimes they do.

Epilogue One

Millie

Four weeks later ...

From the moment we met, Bo and I have been inseparable.

He posted a request that was more like an order on Instagram. He asked for privacy and for people to stop stalking us and to give us space. In return he'd post a photo of us once a week and give a free game pass to a person who posted a photo of themselves doing something kind for someone else. #ShowMeKindness has gone viral, what do you know.

I started an Instagram, too, at Violet's insistence. She said it would be better to have people stalk me online than in person. Turns out, she's right. I've already got a million followers. A bunch of companies have approached me, offering to pay huge amounts of money to have me advertise their products. So far I've agreed to a few and I've already made more money than I ever expected to see in this lifetime.

My book launch went ... very well. It's not hard to google my backstory, which is mainly what the book is about. The headlines sort of made me cringe, but I'm learning that you can't control what people say and it's best to focus on other things.

Bo insists that I have bodyguards when I go out or to my classes. I flat-out refused at first. Until I realized he was right and that people are crazy.

I'm glad he basically lives in a castle with a fortified wall around the entire property. He's had even more intensive security systems installed and it's the one place I actually feel safe.

It's Friday afternoon. I've been working on my new book for over a month now, and it's coming along even better than I expected. If things continue to go this well, I might even be able to get it finished before Thanksgiving.

I miss him. It's been six hours since I last saw Bo, and I'm starting to feel like I always do when I've gone too long without. We've spent every night together since that very first day. It's good that I can keep busy. It's the only way I can bear to be apart from him. I'm so in love with Bo McCabe it's hard to think straight if I don't immerse myself in my writing.

His mother's studio, which is now my studio, is the perfect place to work. As soon as I step through the door, my ideas start to well up, wanting out. Bo put most of his mother's boxes away, but I've hung her garments in the closet and carefully kept everything together. As a tribute, maybe. As a reminder to make the most of every day.

I back-up today's work and put my flash drive into its drawer.

I hear the door open, and there he is. His face lights up as soon as he sees me. Will I ever get used to how stunning he is? How perfect, for me and only me? He's wearing a nice shirt and a blazer and his aviator sunglasses. His hair is windblown. He's carrying a bag, like a carry-on suitcase.

I close my laptop. He slides his glasses up and sets down his bag. He lifts me into his arms. Then he kisses me and it's so lusty and full of love I feel dizzy with happiness.

"You look so fucking gorgeous I want to eat you alive," he says. "But it'll have to wait. Are you ready?"

He has a home game tonight. I always go to his games. When they have away games, Violet and I ride on the team bus with them. His coach even sends catering to our VIP box. For the home games, Violet always makes a party out of it. "What's the bag for?"

"After the game, I'm taking you away for the weekend. To celebrate."

"What are we celebrating?"

"You'll see."

Bo has landed three major endorsements that are worth more money than I can even think about. He's also getting ready for the draft picks. He's been playing *really* well. His team is undefeated and he's been getting a lot of attention. Whatever happens, wherever he ends up, I'll go with him, we've already decided that. It's a little daunting to think about a future with him, but he always makes it sound so easy, and so certain.

He pre-empts my protests. "You've been working non-stop for a month, Millie. You said it yourself, you're ahead of schedule. You need a break. I'm not taking no for an answer, sweetheart."

"But where are we going?"

"It's a surprise."

He takes my hand and leads me to his (now *our*, since I moved in with him the day we met) bedroom. He helps me pack a bag. Then he takes me down to the four-car garage, where his Corvette, his Land Rover, his Ducati and his Porsche live. We take the Corvette.

I'm escorted to the VIP box where Violet is already waiting, with a few friends.

The game starts and Bo does his usual magic, until his team is up 28-3 at half time.

His team runs off the field. But Bo doesn't.

He's still standing there, looking up at the Jumbotron.

One of the other players runs out and hands him a small box and a microphone, before running off again.

"What's he doing?" says Violet. "Oh my God, Millie, look at the Jumbotron."

Oh, God.

It's showing that video of me. The one he stared at. The one that went viral.

The entire stadium goes quiet.

Bo takes off his helmet. He taps the microphone. Then he says into it, "Millie Baylin. Please come down onto the field. There's something I need to ask you."

What?

Violet squeals. "What's he doing? Millie! You have to go down there."

I'm sort of frozen in place but she steers me toward the door of our VIP box.

What *is* he doing?

I walk down the steps of the stadium, my heart beating like a wild thing.

Everyone is watching me.

But I can only see Bo, standing there, waiting for me.

I step down onto the field and we walk toward each other.

Until I'm standing right in front of him. His blue eyes are sparkling with love and something else.

Almost like he's nervous. Which isn't typical for Mr. Quarterback.

He gets down on one knee.

Oh. I feel my hand cover my mouth.

"Millie, I know it's only been a month. And I know we're still young. But I've never been more sure about anything, ever, as I am about how much I love you. I fell in love with you from the very first moment I saw you. I want to be with you. I want to marry you. I want to have babies with you and grow old with you. You're mine and I'm yours and that's never going to change for me. You're the one. Will you marry me, baby?"

I can vaguely hear a hundred thousand people gasp.

Bo opens the small box he's holding, revealing the most beautiful ring I've ever seen. It's two delicate gold bands held together by a row of seven glinting diamonds. I don't need to count them. I know seven is his lucky number. It's the one he wears.

"Yes," I whisper.

He beams at me and slides the ring onto my finger. Then he says into the microphone, "She said yes."

The stadium erupts. It's so loud it sounds like an earthquake.

Bo stands up. He lifts me into his arms and he kisses me. "I was really hoping you'd say yes."

I laugh and I kiss him again.

I didn't know happiness could feel this complete.

After they win the game, we catch our flight to New York. I'm nervous. I've never flown before. But Bo holds my hand the entire way. From the first class cabin, we gaze out at the city skyline as our plane descends into New York City at sunset. I've never seen anything so awe-inspiring.

We check in to our hotel room which happens to be amazing with views out over Manhattan. He takes me up to the penthouse restaurant and bar, where we sit and order drinks.

Even though Bo and I have been practically inseparable ever since we went viral, and even though he makes sweet, scorching-hot love to me every chance we get, I still haven't told him I love him. I don't know why I haven't. I *know* I love him. I guess I've been scared that he'll somehow be taken from me. Maybe it's a fear that was ingrained in me after ... everything that happened.

Bo told me he loved me exactly one week after we met. Now, he tells me he loves me about a hundred times a day.

He doesn't hound me about saying it back. But I know he wants me to.

And now, with his eyes glimmering and the world at our feet, I don't feel scared anymore. I only feel strong. And so full of love for him I just can't hold it in anymore. He's holding my hand, fingering my ring.

"Bo?"

"Yeah?"

"I love you. I can't wait to marry you."

I never thought I'd see it, but the star quarterback has tears in his eyes.

I lean into him, touching my lips against his. It feels so good to finally say it. He takes a hundred dollar bill out of his pocket and leaves it on the table, even though we've only had one drink and haven't ordered our meals yet. He stands up, carefully pulls my chair back and then he scoops me into his arms.

"Bo—"

"I need you right now, baby. I want to hear you say that when I'm inside you."

Oh.

He takes me down to our hotel room. He carries me to the bed and lays me down. Kissing me, he peels off my dress and my panties. His mouth is on my breasts as he tears off his own clothes. *I love you,* he murmurs against my skin. *You break my heart, I love you so much.* Bo's mouth is voracious. He suckles on my nipples until I'm wet and squirming with need. Then he kisses a line down my stomach and pushes my thighs open. He feasts on me with his greedy mouth and pushes his tongue into me, teasing my clit until I come in a warm rush of pleasure. Then he climbs onto me, pushing my knees up. He slides his huge, hot, silky-wet cock inside me, deep, deeper, rooting out pleasure with each driving thrust. I wrap my legs around him, until his thick length fills me inexorably.

He stares into my eyes and I say it. "I love you, Bo. I love you."

Our hands link and he thrusts deeper, possessively, gliding in and out with languid force. His rock-hard cock is relentless, until I'm gasping his name, my hands gripping him with the intensity of my ecstasy.

You're so beautiful, Millie, so perfect to me. I'll never have enough of you. Never. I'll never stop loving you.

I come hard, my body clenching in juicy bursts, tugging at his thick cock until he spills his hot seed deep inside me. He growls my name against my neck. The ripples continue for a long time and Bo keeps thrusting in a lazy rhythm as he kisses me and murmurs his sweet words, prolonging the bliss, until we come again. And again.

We don't end up exploring much of the city's sights. We're too insatiable, too in love to disengage. We order room service and feast on each other the entire weekend. We finally make it to the top of the Empire State Building just a couple of hours before our plane is due to depart. We don't even notice when someone takes a photo of us kissing, with the skyline behind us against a vermillion sunset.

It ends up in The New York Times and a lot of other national newspapers and newsfeeds with the headline, *Hopeless Romantics.*

It's true enough, even though I never thought of myself that way.

Not until Bo changed my mind.

When we get back home, I message Violet and tell her to come over. Bo has practice and she wants to hear about New York. Even though I never did end up spending even one night in our dorm room, we have two classes together so at least we get to spend time together then. And, of course, the football games. We make good use of our VIP box.

When I let her in, she gushes over my ring.

We sit in the hot tub for a while and she talks about the party she went to over the weekend. A lot of guys have been asking her out, but she hasn't agreed to date any of them yet. "I don't know," she sighs. "I'm blaming you and Bo, Millie. *I* want something real. I want someone to sweep me off *my* feet."

"I'm sure you'll find someone. He'll probably show up when you're least expecting it."

"I hope you're right."

After a while, we step out of the hot tub. I hand her a towel from the heated rack and we lay on the loungers in the sun that's pouring in.

We both look up when someone walks into the pool area.

At first I think it's Bo.

He looks like Bo.

But he's clearly *not* Bo.

He's around the same height as Bo and very muscular, but lean. Hard-looking. His hair is cut short, military-style, but it's grown out a little. He's wearing fatigues with the sleeves rolled up. His skin is deeply tanned and he has a lot of ink. Like his brother, he's outrageously handsome, but his dark gray eyes are spooked and haunted-looking. I guess it's not hard to figure out why. From what Bo described, he's seen more combat than anyone should.

"You must be Caleb. Hi, I'm Millie. This is Violet."

"Oh, Bo's brother," Violet says. "The soldier."

Caleb's eyes lock on Violet and she blushes. The pink of her cheeks somehow enhances the bright golden-copper color of her long, thick hair. Her bikini, it has to be said, is on the skimpier side.

"Hi, Caleb," says Violet. "It must feel strange to get home after being away for so long."

Caleb seems lost for words.

He doesn't say anything.

He stares at Violet for a few more seconds, then he turns around and walks out.

That was the day everything changed for Violet, even though there have been more than a few bumps in the road.

As it turns out, Bo isn't the only McCabe brother who, once he falls, falls *hard*.

But that's a story for Violet to tell you herself ...

Epilogue Two

Millie

Two years later ...

Bo was drafted by the Packers and is now their starting quarterback. The stadium is amazing. Watching him play there is beyond a dream. He's so in his element on that field it's just a joy to watch him. As far as his pay check goes, it's just ... a crazy amount of money.

Only two months after we met, we got married in a tiny but wildly romantic ceremony at our house, by the lake. It was the best day of my life. Well, actually, every day I spend with Bo McCabe is the best day of my life. He bought us a house in Green Bay and we divide our time between our two homes. My favorite space is still his mother's studio in the house I adore, with its lake and the rolling hills of our land.

I've now written four books and they've all been New York Times Bestsellers, which is mind-blowing to me. I do a few book signings but not many book tours. I don't like the crowds. And I'd rather be with my husband. He's framed all the write-ups and the lists and they hang on the walls of my studio.

Bo has some time off since it's the off-season and he's gone over to spend some time with his brother.

We've been married now for almost two years.

Bo hints to me every day that he wants me to go off the pill. He wants to fill up the house, he said, with our babies. Even though we're still young, I've decided it's time.

I'm waiting for him to get back. I'm taking a bubble bath. We had the master bedroom and bathroom and a few other areas of the house redone after we got married, so it could be *ours*, he said, and not just his, or his family's. I can't wait to see him, even though he's only been gone for a few hours. It's like my body and soul crave him when we're not together.

I hear the door slam, and his footsteps as he runs up the stairs. "Baby?" he calls out. Then he storms in to our palatial bathroom. A huge smile breaks out on his face, as it always does when he sees me. I smile, too, at my handsome husband. He fills up the room with his male energy and his dazzling presence. "My perfect wife is so damn gorgeous it's blowing my mind." He always talks like this. Like he still can't believe he found me.

"I've been waiting for you," I tell him.

He pulls off his shirt, which messes up his thick hair. His muscles are bigger now than they were when we first met, and they were big even then. He works out all the time and with all the trainers the football team has, his body has been honed into a specimen of prime, beefed-up perfection. He steps out of his jeans. *Wow.* He really is happy to see me. His cock is colossal and rock-hard. He steps into the bath and lowers himself onto me. He's so big he splashes half the water out of the tub and I squeal as he playfully bites my neck.

But then he kisses me and it's a kiss full of devotion and love. He gazes into my eyes. I love how his eyes almost seem to change color depending on his mood. Right now they're as blue as sapphires. "How's my girl? Did you get some writing done?"

"Yes."

I gasp as his massive cock slides against the skin of my thigh. I wrap my arms around his strong neck, letting my fingers glide across the hard, sculpted muscles of his shoulders and arms. I kiss his lips. "There's something I wanted to talk to you about, Bo."

He stares down at me alertly. "Is everything okay?" He's so fiercely protective of me, any sign that I might be unhappy makes him wildly concerned. "What is it?"

"I just wanted to tell you that I went off the pill. I want to have your baby, Bo. I love you so much."

He stares down at me and his expression is layered with raw happiness and deep emotion. And hot, hundred-proof lust. "God, how I love you. I love you so much it makes me fucking crazy." He kisses me, parting my lips with his tongue. "I'm going to give you a baby right now, sweet little wife. I'm going to fill you up with my hot seed all night long until I make a baby in you. Are you ready for me?"

Bo doesn't wait for me to answer him. I guess he can't wait to get on with the task at hand.

He lifts me out of the bath and gently places my feet on the bath mat. As he dries me, he kneels down in front of me and starts licking my pussy. His tongue dips into me, parting my intimate petals. "Mine," he growls. He circles my clit, sucking on me until I moan. His fingers rove and explore, poking silkily into the tiny cove of my ass as his greedy mouth eats my pussy. It's like he *is* going a little crazy. With lust. He's absolutely *ravenous*. His inner caveman is going wild.

My knees go weak but he lifts me up and carries me to our plush, enormous bed.

Bo latches his mouth onto my nipple, playing my breasts with his strong hands. "Soon our baby's going to be sucking on these sweet pink nipples. But he's going to have to share with daddy."

He moves lower. His tongue slides down my stomach and I squirm. He pushes my legs up and open. I let him do whatever he wants. I give myself to him completely, offering myself to him in every way it's possible to do.

"That's my girl," he murmurs, kissing my pussy, parting the silky folds with his tongue. "Do you know how much I fucking love my juicy, gorgeous wife? Every inch of you is my favorite thing in the world, but this part, right here, might be my most favorite of all." He finds the hyper-sensitive nub of my clit and licks it, until I feel the pleasure rushes start to clench deep inside me. But he avoids a rhythm. His tongue circles *around* my clit and it's torture. He's teasing me.

"Bo," I breathe. *"More."*

"You'll get more, sweet baby. You'll get everything you can handle." He continues this delicious torment, bringing me to the brink but not letting me come. "Are you ready for my big cock, sweetheart? Because I'm not letting you come until I'm deep inside you. Those tight little clenches are going to grip my cock while I shoot my cum deep inside you."

He climbs up my body, pushing my knees wide. Then he takes his engorged cock and slides the head of it against my wet pussy, pushing his thickness deep, stretching me and filling me entirely. With his hands, he reaches under me and grabs my ass so I can't retreat even if I wanted to. His weight is bearing down on me but not crushing me. I *love* how big he is. How strong and heavy. His thick cock is stretching me. My body is gripping him tightly. If I wasn't so wet it might almost be painful. But it's not painful. There's only pleasure. Thick, skewering pleasure. His cock is so deep inside me I can feel the broad head of it pushing against my womb.

He's whispering to me as he thrusts into me. With each thrust he doesn't pull back, but lunges deeper. *I worship you, angel. My sweet goddess. My beautiful wife.*

I love you, Bo, I whisper.

He thrusts again, forcing the pleasure higher. And higher. I can feel every rock-hard inch of him and it's the most beautiful thing. The swell of pleasure reaches a high that's so damn good, I try to squirm with the overload, but I can't move. He's gripping me and holding me in place underneath him, forcing me to take it. The wave spreads through me in warm, sweet rushes of pleasure. Succulent spasms grip his big cock in lush tugs, milking every inch of him.

Bo's groaning my name and I feel him: that hot surge of his gushing seed, flooding me and filling me with everything he has to give.

Epilogue Three

Millie

Two years after that ...

Our baby was conceived the very same night I went off the pill. Bo literally would not pull out until he'd come inside me *a lot*. Nine months later to the day, I gave birth to a baby boy. We named him Benjamin Bo Jack McCabe. He's the most beautiful child, with shiny sable-brown hair like his daddy and silver-gray eyes the exact color of mine.

My fifth book came out and it's selling ... exceptionally well. I've done a few book signings, but only in places that are close by, so I can bring Ben and Bo with me. I can't bear to be apart from either one of them, and Ben cries every time I leave him. "I know how you feel, buddy," Bo tells him.

I've already been offered a publishing deal for my next book. The offers just keep getting higher.

I've just come back from a doctor's appointment and Bo is playing with Ben out in the backyard. Bo had a massive playground built when he first found out I was pregnant. He wants lots of babies and I have some news I know will make him happy.

He's running after Ben, who's chasing after a football. But when he sees me, his angelic little face breaks into a huge smile and he forgets about the football and runs straight into my arms. I pick him up and hug him and cover his little face with kisses.

"Daddy wants kisses, too." My gorgeous husband is smiling at me. He takes Ben and holds him in the crook of his burly arm. Bo puts his warm hand on my swollen belly. "How'd it go at the doctor's?"

We decided not to wait too long after Ben was born to try for another baby. It turns out Daddy is *always* up for making babies. It's his favorite thing to do.

"It's twins," I tell him, beaming. "Girls."

Bo's dark eyebrows lift. He's stunned, but then he grins, just like Ben is grinning, even though I'm sure he doesn't know quite what he's in for.

I think about that day when Bo first saw me on the Jumbotron. How he told me he *knew*. I knew it, too, from that very first night. Even though it took me a little longer to admit it to myself. I felt it then and I feel it now, as he kisses me.

We say it at the same time.

I love you.

Dear Reader,

Thank you so much for reading Hopeless Romantic. I hope you enjoyed Bo and Millie's love story!

Reviews are like gold to authors. If you enjoyed Bo and Millie's story, please consider taking a few minutes to leave a review or rating on Amazon.

Xoxo,
Julie Capulet

My Hero

**He's broken. He's beautiful. He's a bastard.
And he's mine.**

Caleb McCabe just returned from a tour of duty in
Afghanistan. He's shell-shocked. Loud noises make him
jump. He feels like an outcast in civilian society. When
Caleb meets a gorgeous, fun-loving redhead named Violet,
he knows he can't handle a relationship, especially with a
golden girl like her. But that doesn't stop him from
thinking about her day and night.

Violet Jameson is studying for a degree in psychology.
When she meets the ultra-hot combat hero Caleb, she's
riveted not only by his rugged good looks but also by his
obvious vulnerabilities. She yearns to get close to him, and
to begin to heal him. They share a night of passion that's so
hot she realizes she's not only in lust but in love.

For Violet's sake, Caleb tries to stay away. He wants her
more than he can bear, but he's afraid of hurting her with
his own emotional scars. The problem is, no matter how
much he fights his obsession, he can't stop himself. He has
to make her his. He knows in his heart she's the one.

Caleb and Violet are meant for each other, but will his dark
damages get in the way of their Happily Ever After?

My Hero is a sexy standalone novella starring a battle-
scarred alpha hero and the sweet, sassy redhead who
changes everything.

Book 2 in the McCabe Brothers Series

Chapter One

"Today's topic is ..." My psychology professor starts writing some words on the whiteboard. " ... Post Traumatic Stress Disorder, which is, as suggested, triggered by a life event that has in some way been traumatic. Today we'll talk about the causes that can lead to PTSD."

I'm riveted, as usual. I wish I could say there are days that Professor Jackson's lectures are boring, when I find myself staring out the window while I daydream about football players, like a normal person would. This isn't quite the case (okay, sometimes I daydream about football players).

In every other area of my life, I'm an outgoing, fun-loving party girl. But when it comes to the study of psychology, I'm a total nerd. I've known I wanted to be a shrink since I was around seven years old, which is probably pretty weird. Who knows they want to be a psychoanalyst when they're seven years old?

Me, as it turns out.

I have three older brothers. I used to use them as my patients, which they of course hated. But there was no escaping me. I made them lie on the couch while I worked through my list of questions, solving all their problems. To this day, they refuse to sit on a couch in the same room as me. But all three of them are well-adjusted, mostly-happy, highly-paid professionals with degrees and nice girlfriends, so I like to think I had something to do with all that.

Now, I'm a freshman studying—you guessed it—psychology. I'm only about a month in, and I'm already loving it. My plan is to be a licensed psychotherapist by the time I'm twenty-seven. A weird aspiration, possibly, but that's just me. Along the way, though, I also plan on having a fabulous time. Also me. I'm one of those people that can't *not* have a good time. Some people call me "bubbly," "extroverted," "a social butterfly," etc. I like to have fun. I figure that's not a bad thing, so I just go with it.

Professor Jackson continues. "People with PTSD may experience a variety of symptoms including ... " More writing on the white board. "Violet, would you please read out this list?" Professor Jackson loves my enthusiasm.

So I read out the list.

1) Feeling emotionally numb
2) Feeling detached from family and friends
3) Having difficulty maintaining close relationships
4) Lacking interest in activities they once enjoyed

"Thank you, Violet," says Professor Jackson. "Class, your homework for Monday is to read pages 223 to 405, which cover these and other symptoms."

I've already read the textbook, and I've already read widely about PTSD, in detail. It must be a terrible thing to go through, and it makes me feel grateful.

I'm lucky.

My life has been outrageously trauma-free so far. (Except for one thing, which I prefer not to dwell on.) My parents are happily married and still live in our family home back in Wilmington. My three brothers are rowdy, fun, awesome people. They're basically my own personal bodyguards, support network and best friends. When my phone buzzes in my pocket, it's usually one of them, checking up on me, like they do on practically an hourly basis.

My phone buzzes in my pocket.

Will it be Liam, Henry or Aiden this time?

Come over to Bo's after your class and hang out with me.

Not my brothers. It's a snap from my new roommate, Millie. Things have been a little crazy for her lately because she just so happens to have hooked up with the star freaking quarterback and is now practically living with him.

Once they got started, it became *very* intense *very* quickly, which is why it's been so crazy.

I convinced her to come with me to the first game of the season, on our very first day at school. There we were, innocently watching the game, getting to know each other, minding our own business ... and that's when it happened. The über-hot quarterback glanced up at the Jumbotron, which was, in that moment, zeroed in on Millie. She's gorgeous but sort of tries to hide it because she's shy AF. But the cameraperson just stayed on her as a gust of wind blew her hat off, letting loose her hair, which is a really unusual and amazing shade of pale reddish-blond. I don't know why she keeps it hidden all the time, but she always wears it tucked into her hat. And suddenly there it was in all its golden glory, dramatic and glowing under the spotlights on the big screen. The quarterback froze in place like he was starstruck, for so long that everyone in the stands also turned to look at what *he* was looking at. And then it became this *event* because everyone was wondering who this beautiful, mysterious girl was that had brought the quarterback and the entire game to a standstill. By then, the coach was going ballistic and Bo almost got taken off because he was so distracted. But he managed to get it together and they won the game. Which we missed the end of, because Millie was mortified and insisted on leaving. Everyone was staring at her and she hates that kind of attention, so I went back to the dorm with her to make sure she was okay.

But then, within less than an hour, the whole thing went viral. One of Bo's friends, another football player, had posted something about how Bo was looking for Millie, who'd by then been dubbed "the Jumbotron Angel" and it was all #BoWantsTo Know and so on.

Long story short, with the help of basically the entire campus, Bo's team ended up tracking her down. It took him a while to find her, but once he did, they went from zero to sixty pretty fast.

They're perfect for each other, you can just tell. I'm not an expert at matchmaking or anything, but it's just a fact. You can see it by the way they gaze at each other in this annoyingly (in a good way and basically in the kind of way you wish *you* were gazing at someone) loved-up kind of way.

Anyway, I haven't seen a lot of Millie since all that happened. Most likely, she's in Bo's to-die-for mansion.

Even though Millie and I haven't known each other that long, and she never even ended up spending a single night in our dorm room, we really clicked, and I miss her.

A lot of people would be happy to have their own room. I just don't happen to be one of them. Growing up as the youngest of four (actually five, but that's a story for another day), we always had a lot of people coming and going in our house. My parents are both social people and my brothers always had a lot of girls chasing after them, coming around and hanging out. And my mom likes to cook so is always putting on little impromptu parties for everyone that comes over. And my brothers are big and loud and have a lot of stuff everywhere, so there's always a lot of people and activity and fun, which I thrive on.

Sitting in my empty dorm room all alone sucks. I don't really want to go back there after class to stare at the four walls. I've already done my homework, because, as mentioned, I'm obsessed and have already read my psych textbooks from cover to cover.

So when I see Millie's snap of her sitting in a hot tub—*Bo has practice so I'm all alone. I need you!*—my afternoon plans slide into place. Bo's house is incredible. His parents died a few years ago, I'm not sure how. Millie said Bo has two older brothers. One is a CEO of his own company and the other one is in the military. He's been in Afghanistan for a year, she said.

Shit, is what I was thinking.

I really can't imagine going to war. I admire the hell out of those people, putting themselves on the line like that.

Professor Jackson is still talking. "Most people who go through these traumatic events have difficulty adjusting to normal life. They might have trouble talking to people in normal social situations. They often have a hard time adjusting and coping. If left untreated, their symptoms can last for years, or even a lifetime. But with good care and good self-care, they *can* get better, often much better."

Another snap from Millie. *When are you coming?!?*

I message her back. *My class finishes in ten. I'll be right over.*

Chapter Two

CALEB

"*McCabe! You've been given a direct order! Leave him! Return to your post immediately. There's nothing more you can do here! This soldier is dead. Let the medics take him.*"

It can't be true. My three closest friends in this hell have all been killed within the past three days. They call me one of the best snipers we have, but it makes no difference. I pick them off, but it makes no difference. I follow orders, but it makes no difference. My men get shot anyway. Their brains splatter against dusty, shell-pocked walls and their blood spills onto the ground like thick dark-red oil. It's all over me. And then I realize it's not Logan's blood that's all over me. It's mine.

I'm glad.

I want it to be mine. I want to trade my blood for Logan's. I want to rewind time and take his bullet. I want his blood to ooze back into him, so he wakes up and cracks another joke. Why should I live if he can't?

My pain feels good. So fucking deserved. And when oblivion overtakes me, it's the most peaceful feeling I've had in an entire goddamn year.

"Excuse me, mister?" Someone's tapping me on the shoulder. "Mister?"

I jerk awake and some kid is staring at me over the seats of the bus. My hands feel empty and I realize it's because I'm not clutching my rifle.

It takes me a second to get my bearings. I'm on a bus. I'm on my way home. I've been discharged. I'm mostly recovered. I spent the last month in a military hospital. Now I'm back on American soil. I'm alive and I'm not holding an M4 carbine.

"I think you were having a nightmare," says the kid.

I don't respond. I just turn away from him and look out the window.

Thankfully, he goes away, putting his earbuds back in and scrolling on his phone. Thank fuck. I'm hardly going to explain to some clueless kid about my "nightmare." My whole fucking *life* is a nightmare. I can't get away from it. It fills my dreams and every waking second. It's all I can think about. It consumes me, like I'm being eaten alive by my gruesomely-detailed memories.

The landscape looks the same. Vast. Greener than the desert. More neon and plastic and brick. More slow-paced normality, if there is such a thing. We pull into the bus station and I pick up my duffle bag. I grab a taxi and give the driver the address. The last thing I feel like doing is talking, so I don't, even though the taxi driver rambles on about something I don't care about. I can hardly bear the familiarity of my neighborhood as we drive through it. Everything is the same—yet nothing will ever be the same. How can it be? The contradictions hurt my head and my heart so deeply, for a second I'm wondering if I'm having a heart attack.

Unfortunately, I'm not.

We pull up in front of my gate and I pay the guy. He thanks me gushingly and I realize I've given him a two hundred percent tip. He looks so happy, I tell him to keep it, and I wonder if I'll ever feel that emotion again. *Happy.* The word itself annoys me. None of *them* will ever feel happy again. And neither will I.

I remember the code for the gate, even though it's not something I've thought about for a year. I walk up the driveway. It looks nice. It's a beautiful place, I can vaguely recognize.

The front door of my house is unlocked, which is good, since I don't have a key. Gage emailed, saying he'll be in town as soon as he can. He's got a company takeover or something but says he wants to see me. Bo will be around but is probably at practice. I remember how intense the coaches work you. I used to be on the team. An all-star, not that it matters at this point. My injuries mean that I'll never play ball again, not that I would want to at this point.

All that feels like a long time ago.

An easier time, before daggers of sorrow became everything.

I hear voices coming from the pool area.

Girls' voices.

I drop my duffle bag and step through the door, wondering if Bo is with them.

Two girls in bikinis are lying on loungers.

They both stare at me and I stare back.

My brain can't quite handle this. I haven't seen a girl in a bikini—or any woman for that matter who isn't a war-hardened soldier in combat fatigues—for a very long time. They're both gorgeous, especially the one with the long, copper-bright hair and the white bikini, the curvier one, the one who's smiling and was laughing until I stepped into view. The other girl, who has very pale red-blond hair, says, "You must be Caleb. Hi, I'm Millie. This is Violet."

It's strange to hear my name. No one's called me anything but McCabe since I left for Afghanistan.

"Oh. Bo's brother," says the redhead. "The soldier." She stands up and starts walking over to me. She has bright green eyes and a sprinkling of golden freckles across her nose. Her face reminds me of that word again: *happy*. In fact I don't think I've ever seen a person who sort of *radiates* happiness as much as this girl does. My eyes want to drink in all that golden skin and the long legs and mind-numbing curves, barely covered at all by those tiny shreds of wet white fabric. That dazzling, welcoming, delighted smile.

But I can't even look. This is *way* too much.

I can't handle it. If she touches me, I might fucking self-combust. Every nerve ending in my body is crackling, like I'm about to get a severe, hot electric shock that could very possibly jolt me over the edge of sanity.

I take a step back.

Her smile falters a little as she notices my reaction. But she holds her ground. She's not intimidated like the other girl seems to be, who's also standing up now but keeping her distance. I probably weigh as much as both of them, plus one, put together. All we do in our downtime is sleep, train and work out and I'm basically a hard, ruthless fighting machine at this point.

"Hi, Caleb," says the dazzling girl, and I see now that her hair is a bright shade of red but has also has all these other shades of gold and deeper reds and strawberry blond in it, too, like she's been painted all the colors of the sun. Her green eyes have shards of lighter, off-neon green and gold in them, as though she's plugged in. Her lips are a heart-breaking shade of pink. She's just so freakishly ... *colorful,* in every possible way. I have the urge to shade my eyes from her. "It must feel strange to get home after being away for so long." She's talking to me carefully. Her voice is almost soothing—if I were capable of being soothed.

The problem is, I'm not.

The only thing I'm capable of being is one hundred percent fucked up.

So I take another step back. I don't even reply to her. I can't bring myself to say anything at all.

I return to the coolness of the house, relieved to be away from all that ... *glory*. That smile and all that bouncy softness and warm skin and, basically, way the fuck too much of everything. Details that belong to a place I'm a long way away from. Heaven, maybe. Heaven on earth.

I walk to the fridge and drink all the orange juice straight out of the container. Then I go upstairs to my old room, which—incredibly—is entirely unchanged. I strip down to my boxers, throw my fatigues over a chair, and reach to pull the curtains closed. I need some sweet relief from the overly sunny daylight. Before I can fully close the curtains, though, I notice the two girls are getting into the redhead's car. My movement catches her eye and she looks up.

She looks so healthy and perfect and beautiful in her tight jeans and her pink sweater that I feel like I'm having another one of those heart attacks. She's a goddess. A pure, undamaged dream. There's no way in hell I would ever inflict her with my own scars or dirty her with the fucked-up mess I've become. I wouldn't even consider it.

I don't know if there's any hope for me at this point. I'm too far gone.

I pull the curtains closed, blocking her from view. Then I crawl into bed, where I plan to stay for a long time. I feel like I haven't slept—really slept—in years.

Even so, my mind retraces the colors of her hair, the golden smoothness of her skin, sparkling with drops of glinting water. The taut little peaks of her nipples under that ridiculously-skimpy bikini.

How easy it would have been to rip off those tiny shreds of fabric ... with hardly any effort at all.

The car starts up loudly, startling me, the noise reminding me of diesel fumes and the smell of gunpowder. Dust. Pain. Blood.

Every memory and every detail cuts deeper into my regret. I gave it every fucking thing I had, and I still couldn't save them.

Much later, somehow, I fall into the blissful darkness of sleep. All I really want to do is stay there ...

Arrogant Player

He's ruthless. And he won't stop until he has her right where he wants her.

Luna LaRoux has poured her heart and soul into her waterfront bar and restaurant, which has the best sunsets in Key West. The only problem is, Luna's best friend and business partner Josie is having money problems, and with twins on the way, Josie has no choice but to sell her half of the business. Actually, it's 51%.

Gage McCabe is spending the weekend in Key West when he happens to overhear an interesting conversation. Between a very pregnant majority shareholder and her stunningly beautiful—and deliciously desperate—business partner.

Gage can't resist. The bar is obviously a thriving business, and his new partner will just have to get used to *him* calling the shots ... if she doesn't kill him first. It's this detail that frustrates him the most: she seems entirely immune to his charms. Unheard of. Gage is so sure of his own allure, he bets Luna his share that she'll surrender to him within a month—or the bar is hers.

Perfect. All Luna has to do is resist his drop-dead gorgeous looks, his smug charisma and his impressive ... endowments, then she'll be rid of him for good. Easy, right?

Arrogant Player is a sexy standalone enemies-to-lovers romance starring an alpha playboy and the one woman he can't control ... or stay away from.

Book 3 in the McCabe Brothers Series

248

Nashville Days

It's the hottest summer on record …

Travis Tucker is the lead singer in a country-rock band whose four albums have all hit number one. Life as a superstar is good. The only problem is, he gets swarmed wherever he goes. So he decides to buy himself a secret country getaway to work on his next record and clear his head.

Ruby Hayes is on a mission. Nothing is going to stop her from fulfilling her dream of making it as a singer and songwriter. She'll spend the summer writing songs on the grand piano in the abandoned farmhouse next door. Then she's on her way to Nashville.

When Travis finds Ruby, singing like an angel at his piano, she ignites a wild obsession and an all-consuming lust that will make this summer the hottest on record.

But will Ruby's ambition, a jealous best friend and the demands of Travis's high-profile life come between them? Or is this a match made in country music heaven?

Nashville Days is a sexy standalone romance starring a hot alpha rock star and the sweet, sassy songbird who steals his heart.

Music City Lovers series

ALSO BY JULIE CAPULET

Nashville Nights

He's crazy for her ...

Vaughn Tucker is the hot playboy drummer of the Tucker Brothers band, whose four albums have all hit number one. Vaughn is drop-dead gorgeous ... and completely out of control.

Vaughn Tucker is the hot playboy drummer of the Tucker Brothers band, whose four albums have all hit number one. Vaughn is drop-dead gorgeous ... and completely out of control.

Gigi Hayes's life is a million miles from packed stadiums and high-profile tour schedules. She's a small-town girl who spends all her time working in the library and studying to become a qualified social worker. For ... reasons.

When Vaughn meets Gigi, for the first time in his life, he's the one who's star-struck. But Gigi is saving herself for true love. And even though she's drawn, against her will, to the beautiful, trouble-written-all-over-him superstar, she's not deluded enough to believe he's capable of such a thing.

Vaughn has already fallen hard. And Gigi's refusals only make him crazier. She's an angel and he may as well be the devil himself. But when heaven meets hell, all bets are off ...

Nashville Nights is a sexy standalone romance starring an out-of-control alpha musician and the one woman who's everything he never knew he needed.

Music City Lovers Series

Nashville Dreams

"All I wished for was to experience that spark you read about, just once. What I wasn't expecting was the Fourth of July and heaven on earth all rolled into one." ~ Stella

Bass player Kade Tucker is known as the Magic Man, and not only for his riffs. After breaking off a disastrous relationship, he swears off women. Only problem is, five minutes later, he might have just met the love of his life.

Stella Bell has always done what's expected of her. Until a secret letter and an unexpected proposal on the same day prove to be her breaking point. For once in her life, she's going to do something for herself. As fate would have it, that means taking a spur of the moment trip to Nashville.

A hopeless romantic, Stella has been hiding her true self for far too long. And when a gorgeous, mysterious stranger rescues her from a torrential downpour, she decides to go with it. The hot, dreamy Kade Tucker proceeds to enlighten Stella in every possible way, until she begins to realize that some dreams really can come true.

But will Kade's twisted ex and Stella's family secrets -- along with a very accidental pregnancy -- get in the way of their HEA? Or is this a star-crossed match made in Music City heaven?

Nashville Dreams is a super-sexy standalone rock star romance starring a hot alpha musician and a sweet & sassy dreamer who's the one he always knew was out there somewhere. Now that he's found her, he has no intention of letting any one of her dreams go unanswered.

Music City Lovers series

Book 1 in the I Love You series

XOXO I Love You

A young graduate. A ruthless CEO. And an attraction neither of them was prepared for.

Somehow I got an interview at Downtown, the "It" company of the decade.
Sure, I'd heard the rumors about the CEO, Rafe Black.
How elusive he was. How rich. How *hot*.

None of it prepared me for what was about to happen. The white-hot lust at first sight. The attraction that wasn't just mutual but obsessive, life-changing and enough to test the limits of what I could handle ...

XOXO I Love You is the first book in the I Love You series. If you like fun, sexy romance starring obsessed alphas, you'll love Julie Capulet's page-turning book.

Book 2 in the I Love You series

XOXX I Love You More

Lexi and Rafe's connection began with an intense lust and a white-hot obsession. Then it deepened into an all-encompassing love affair that awes them both. But when Rafe's jealousy reaches fever-pitch, it only drives Lexi away ... and literally into the arms of Rafe's rebel brother, Max.

Will Rafe find her? Will Max cross a line? And can Lexi forgive Rafe for loving her too much?

Their tangled web only gets more complicated as Lexi returns to Downtown to begin her new job. Rafe has to somehow figure out how to balance his love with his overprotective urges. But will an ex from Rafe's past and a colleague who has his sights set on the CEO's gorgeous new assistant be enough to drive them apart again?

Or are Rafe and Lexi destined to be together?

Find out in the exciting conclusion to the I Love You series duet (includes an epilogue!).

MAX

I notice him as soon as he walks into my restaurant. Of course I do. He's buff as hell, with tattoos and a dark, pirate-king vibe. He's wearing a black leather jacket over his business shirt. And he's the sexiest man I've ever seen.

He's also wearing one of those criminal cuffs on his left wrist.

Just what I don't need. A rich bad boy with rage issues. It's scary enough that one of my customers has turned into a stalker.

But when the stalker follows me home one night, it's *him* who shows up exactly when I need him to — the gorgeous blue-eyed stranger who could be either the devil or a saint.

And there's more to Max Black than I could have ever imagined. Turns out the worst kind of bad boy can also be the most beautiful savior. He's scarred by his dark past, but underneath the tough exterior is the biggest ... heart. And the tenderest soul. He's a renegade angel and a white knight. And the one true love of my life.

Max is a spin-off from the I Love You series and is a sexy standalone story.

Cowboy

He's about to meet the unexpected city girl who brings him to his knees ...

Will Finn is a rodeo hero from Montana. After getting thrown and trampled by a rampaging bull six months ago, he just made his comeback in the ring. But out of it, he seems distracted – even though every woman in Bozeman wants a piece of him.

Ella Parker is an art curator from New York City who's about to lose her job and possibly her apartment. She's as desperate as desperate gets. If she can just find *one* outstandingly talented artist, she'll finally be able to realize her dream of starting her own gallery. And when work takes her to Bozeman for an exhibition, she stumbles across a discovery that has the potential to change her life.

As their paths collide, Will and Ella find that each has something the other wants. But neither is about to give in easily, especially when sparks begin not just to fly but to ignite them both in ways they never even imagined ...

Cowboy is a sexy standalone opposites-attract romance starring a hot alpha rodeo hero and the sweet & sassy New Yorker who's the very last thing he expected ... his new obsession, his true love and his muse (includes two OTT steamy and romantic HEA epilogues!).

ABOUT THE AUTHOR

Julie Capulet writes contemporary romance starring sexy, obsessed alphas and the sweet & sassy women who bring them to their knees. Her stories are inspired by true love and she's married to her own real life hero. When she's not writing, she's reading, walking on the beach, drinking wine and watching rom-coms.

www.juliecapulet.com

Printed in Great Britain
by Amazon

87166989R00148